Capturing the Orc's Heart

Trollkin Lovers

Book Three

Lyonne Riley

CHAPTER 1

ZIRELLE

There's a new guy coming in today, or so they tell me.

"Be nice, Captain," Corporal Jar'kel says.

I give him a withering smile. "I'm always nice." We both know this isn't true, but the one-tusked troll doesn't argue. I might be human, but he's still my underling, and he knows better by now.

"However..." Jar'kel sniffs the air. "You reek like alcohol today. Perhaps this is not the best way to greet the new lieutenant."

Right. Last night I stayed out drinking until I'd forgotten all about the pile of paperwork waiting for me on my desk. When my mind was finally numb and quiet, I stumbled back to my little house outside the barracks and passed out in my hammock. That's not helping me much this morning. My head is still hammering, and my blood feels too thick, but it was worth it just for the rare sense of calm I managed to feel without the needs of this great city hanging over my head.

That's the cost of the position that I wanted so much, and I will keep paying the toll.

I sigh. "The lieutenant's going to be here regardless of how I smell. There's nothing to do about it now." I sign off on some papers and add them to the outgoing pile. "Where's he coming from?"

Jar'kel shakes his head, clearly unhappy with what he's about to say. "The frontier. Part of the expansion effort."

That's just lovely. Though tensions in Attirex have eased a little since the war officially ended, we humans won't forget how the trollkin razed our towns to the ground. And yet I have to treat them as if none of this happened. Here in the city guard, we are a part of our respective nations and yet separate. Even if our peoples fight, we don't. That's the agreement—but it doesn't mean we have to like each other. As long as we do our jobs, we can keep the peace in our city.

"It's time," Jar'kel says. "He should be arriving any minute."

With a grunt of acknowledgment, I rise from my chair and we make our way to the ancient throne room, where some monarch ruled over the Hazrain once upon a time.

Recently, a bitchy old trolless retired, vacating her position. It's critical to keep a balance of humans and trollkin on staff, so now they're bringing in her replacement. I know the position's been hard to fill with all the best recruits out on the frontier, occupying their new stolen territories. Whoever we get will be someone who wasn't wanted anywhere else in the Grand Chieftain's empire, so I have very low expectations.

I'm surprised at who walks in the room.

He's big, bigger than any orc I've ever seen, with both sides of his head shaved and his hair pulled up in a high topknot, which makes him look even taller. He has a commanding face, with a big square jaw and sculpted cheekbones, and large tusks that pull up his lips on either side of his mouth. He looks on the young side for his rank, but his uniform is covered in patches and medals. He's accomplished a lot in spite of his youth.

Right away I'm certain that this new orc lieutenant will not be a positive addition to our team. From his walk, from his posture when he comes to a halt in front of us, I can tell he has an ego on him.

And he has a haunted look in his eyes I don't like.

"Welcome," I say in Trollkin, his native language, and hold out my hand. As the first in command, it's my job to begin the introductions. I expect him to say the token *thank you*, spoken in Freysian, back to me.

"Thank you," the lieutenant says—in Trollkin. I glare at Corporal Jar'kel. These are the rules. This is how we acknowledge one another's place here and our agreement to keep the peace together.

"The lieutenant doesn't speak any Freysian," Jar'kel dutifully explains.

I huff. "You brought me someone who can't even talk to half the locals?"

The lieutenant glances between us, irritated that we're talking around him.

"You will have to learn how to speak Freysian to do your job properly," I say in his native tongue, leveling a glare on him. "What was your name?"

He bristles all over, but he'll understand soon enough that even though I'm human, I'm still his superior, and not even an impertinent look in someone's eye is acceptable to me. We run a tight ship in the Attirex guard.

"Agkar," the orc says, lips tight. "Lieutenant Agkar."

"Lieutenant Agkar." I give him a curt nod. "Welcome to the Hazrain. May your sword stay sharp and your armor never rust." It's a traditional greeting here in the desert, where we are constantly pelted by the wind and rough sands.

"Thank you for the warm welcome, sir." I know he's only saying it because he has to. "I look forward to working with you."

AGKAR

It was one of the most bald-faced lies I'd ever told. *I look forward to working with you.* There's nothing I look forward to less than working side-by-side with this woman. This *human* woman.

Captain Zirelle Mastair. She carries a coldness in her nearly black eyes that I return in kind. She has deep brown skin and curly hair, and holds herself with a superiority that immediately grates on me. I will not be looked down upon by a human like I'm a dog to do her bidding.

She wants me to learn to speak her tongue, too, as if I would ever stoop to wrap my mouth around those slippery syllables. This captain is sadly mistaken if she thinks I'm here for language lessons.

Now that the formalities are over with and we've all shaken hands, it's time to get to work. At least I can lose myself in that.

I must admit that despite having to trek through the endless desert to reach it, Attirex is a beautiful city. Crimson and emerald tents spread across the sand like a great blossoming flower, teeming with activity. Everything is decorated with gold, from the canopies to the statues to the women. Orcs, trolls, and humans alike wear earrings of gold, necklaces of gold, bracelets and anklets and rings of gold. There is an unexpected, mysterious beauty to the low-set, clay buildings and high, curved archways. The whole city breathes as if it were alive.

As I travel down rows and rows of tents, I pick up a scent I've never smelled before—something spicy and sweet and a little herbal that seems to emanate from everywhere and nowhere at once. It's so unlike anything I've experienced that for a moment, I forget about the loss and dishonor that led me here. I'm swallowed up by the strangeness of it, the beauty of it, the exotic and foreign idea of humans and trollkin both traversing the same streets and visiting the same shops.

I thought that perhaps, in this great, bustling city, I might be able to find peace. Perhaps I could abandon this sick feeling in my chest and discover my salvation—but after meeting the captain today, I have my doubts.

My very first task is paperwork, of all things. Hundreds of shipments travel through Attirex every day, and some are brought here and searched for goods that might raise the alarm. I'll be made aware of any suspicious cargo and asked to weigh in on what should be done with it. Mostly, we want to ensure people paid their taxes, as that is what supports our efforts here to keep the peace in the first place. On top of playing lawman, I also get to be a glorified tax collector.

Thrilling.

Fights break out frequently between humans and trollkin around the city—as expected—and it's up to the city guard to quell them. Repeat offenders end up in the stocks for everyone to see and mock and occasionally, they even throw produce. Humiliation is one of the best deterrents.

We're also tasked with keeping tabs on the various criminal elements that call Attirex home. They lurk beneath the city, only emerging to take advantage of merchant caravans and smuggle goods in and out. It's a constant drain on us to search the tunnels and monitor known hideouts.

I've only been on the job a week when I hear the captain call over my shoulder. "Ah, Lieutenant." It's hard to mistake her voice—the tenor isn't deep, but it has a richness that can carry a long distance without being loud. "The very orc I've been looking for."

I turn around, not even attempting to mask my annoyance at the interruption. I've already been introduced to the captain's style. She likes to have her hands in a little bit of everything, micromanaging us into doing each task exactly to her specifications. It's a thorn in my side I can't pull out. I already miss Gagzen, the frontier town where I was the top of the food chain and I could run my ship however I chose. I didn't bother my soldiers as long as they completed their duties. Captain Mastair won't even let us take a break unless it's scheduled.

"Hello, Captain," I say in Trollkin, smirking down at her. It's hard to be intimidated when I stand a solid foot and a half taller than she does. "How can I help you?"

A twitch under her eye is all the clue I get that she's annoyed by my impertinent tone.

"You're needed out in the slum rows," she says. "We have eyes on the Hookclaw boss, and once we take him in, I need you and your team to grab all of his underlings, too. Can't let any of the rats scurry away into the darkness."

I'm already familiar with the Hookclaw crime family. My subordinates know them as untouchables, who move goods—particularly dangerous goods, like the green salt—through Attirex, all while flying under the radar. No one's been able to pin their leaders down, just a crony here and there.

"The slum rows?" I ask. Why would she choose me for this petty task, and not one of the officers? Ah, perhaps I know why. They're almost all human, but the captain gets off on bossing trollkin around and giving us the shit jobs.

"Yes, you heard me. The Hookclaws' minions are hunkered down in a few of the shacks down there. You'll need to start the raid when you hear the signal."

I get to my feet and drape my sword belt around my waist. "Fine," I say, and head for the door.

"Fine?" The Captain's voice is pinched. "I think you're missing something."

A snarl sits just inside my mouth. "Fine," I repeat. "*Sir.*"

"Good."

I storm out of the room. Back in Gagzen, I was the word of law, and no one would have ever dared speak to me the way she does. I left hoping to forget, but now I'm not sure coming here has really improved my lot in life.

As much as it grates on me to follow the captain's orders, I find myself in the slum rows with a small team, ready to act when we hear the signal. I am a soldier, after all. I do what I'm told whether I agree with it or not.

We've camped across from the three locations where we're certain Hookclaws are hiding, hands waiting on the hilts of our swords. Then we hear it: The clang of a great gong echoes from one of the guard towers, and it's time to move.

I call out the order to storm the shacks, and all at once we blow past the residents for the back rooms. Sure enough, our guys are playing cards, and they jump to their feet when we break down the door. It doesn't take long for my team to round them all up and tie their hands behind their backs.

That's when a human hiding in a closet jumps out. His frantic eyes search for an escape route, and as he sprints out the nearest exit, I'm right on his heels. With a full-body tackle, I bring him to the ground.

"There's no way out for you," I growl, dragging him back to the house. Then we corral all of them off to jail.

The captain is waiting when we return. She and her team nabbed the Hookclaw family leaders successfully, and she gives a stiff nod of approval as we fill up the rest of the cells with their henchmen.

"Good," she says. "None of the rats got away?"

"One tried," I say. "But I brought him down before he got far."

A small smile lifts the corner of her mouth. "I knew you were the right choice for the job, Lieutenant."

I stand up a little straighter. The captain saw how efficiently we worked today. She even smiled.

The surge of pride I feel is sudden, and I shake it off just as quickly. I did what I did today because it was my job—nothing more, nothing less.

Captain Mastair turns around and claps her hands together high over her head. "Congratulations, everyone. The Hookclaws are a thing of the past, thanks to you!"

A cheer goes up from the assembled guard, but I find my gaze stuck on the captain. For all her enthusiasm, there are deep bags under her eyes, as if she hasn't truly slept in weeks. And yet she's so composed, so firm and self-assured during the day. What is it that has her so exhausted?

I shake my head and leave the little celebration as fast as possible. I don't need to spend a single thought on a human, not again.

CHAPTER 2

ZIRELLE

I'm already having a hard time with the new orc on staff. He's obstinate, and refuses to speak to me with customary respect unless reminded. It's his penchant for taking everything at his own pace that I find deeply irritating. My day is based around productivity. I never leave something undone, and there is much to be done overseeing a city of this size. Even if it means staying late into the night, I won't rest until every day's work is complete. That's how I rose to the rank of captain, anyway, and it's how I'll remain here. I have no partner, no friends, and no family. This is my life. I've thrown all my chips in with the city guard.

So I find it particularly frustrating that not only is Lieutenant Agkar insubordinate, but he carries a commanding air around with him without even trying, when I have to try so hard. His voice booms, and he always seems to take up the entire space he's in. His gold-green eyes are especially to my disliking; I hate the way they squint when I give him an order as if he's biting back what he'd rather say.

Why did he leave the war front in the first place when he hates being here so much? Why would a decorated lieutenant, who came with glowing recommendations from his commander, elect to live in a barren desert that he clearly despises?

"Captain."

I look up to find the very same maddening subject of my thoughts looming in the doorway to my office. He's about to step inside when I raise a hand.

"Always ask before you enter," I say, as if to a child. It's a common courtesy, and not a particularly difficult one to master.

The lieutenant rolls his eyes, not even trying to mask his distaste. "May I come in?" The words are laced with sarcasm.

I don't fall for his bait, though, and simply gesture for him to come inside. "Please."

He steps through, and stands awkwardly in front of my desk. His shoulders are tight, as if he hates being here as much as I do. "We found him."

"Found who?" I ask, tapping my quill.

He unrolls a piece of paper and holds it up. It's an artist's rendering of the Black Fox, a thief responsible for raiding three different shops last week. He's been a thorn in Attirex's side—and by that I mean my side—for months now. He comes out, swipes an entire store's inventory, then goes back into hiding without leaving a trace. How he does it is a mystery to all of us.

"Where is he?" I ask, trying not to let the eagerness slip into my voice. After the last attack, I tasked everyone with digging up information about our robber. Just knowing he's out there, operating right under my nose, keeps me up at night.

"He was seen fleeing into the desert after his last hit," the lieutenant says. "That's why we couldn't find him—he only comes into the city every so often."

"That's all?" I ask, irritation creeping into my voice. "You know that he's in the desert?" What a waste of my time.

The lieutenant frowns, like he's disappointed I'm not happier with this news. "It's a solid lead."

He still can't seem to remember his basic manners. "Sir," I add.

The lieutenant growls. "It's a solid lead, *sir*."

I shake my head. This doesn't help me one bit. "The Hazrain is vast, Lieutenant. He could be anywhere."

"At least we know which direction he went. That's significant." There's some heat bubbling up inside him—that incurable obstinance of his. "With a heading, we could send a search party out into the desert and fan out."

I don't like it, but his proposal is reasonable. We might have a slim shot at finding the Fox, unless he intentionally zigzagged to put us off the scent.

"What if it's a decoy?" I ask. "What if we end up searching in the wrong place?"

"Then we search in the wrong place. But perhaps our presence will frighten him enough that he moves on."

Another good point. I search Agkar's face. Really, for an orc face, it isn't bad. His brows are sharp, less thick and protruding than other trollkin. His tusks are almost delicate, but his facial structure isn't. He has a proud nose and generous lips.

He's also more intelligent than I gave him credit for.

"I suppose I can't argue with your reasoning," I say. His eyebrows fly up with surprise. "All right. Send a party."

"Captain?" He seems confused. "Me? Sir?"

It's clear he didn't expect me to agree with him, and I like keeping him on his toes. "You said it yourself. Perhaps it will drive the Black Fox away to know we've picked up his scent and we're out there looking for him." I tap some papers on my desk. "I leave selecting the team up to you, Lieutenant. Pick whomever you want to go on your little desert adventure."

This earns a perplexed frown from Agkar, which I rather enjoy. I like to think I am a fair captain with the best interests of all in mind. Perhaps he'll see that now.

"Yes, sir," the lieutenant says. But he doesn't turn to leave. When I look back up from my paper, which I still haven't stamped, the orc has a thoughtful look on his face.

"What is it?" I snap.

"You," he says with a sly smile. "I put you on the team, Captain."

AGKAR

I smell alcohol on her today. Her weak human nose must not be able to detect it, but mine does. So our high and mighty Captain Mastair has a weakness after all: The drink.

Against all my expectations, however, she heard out my case—even agreed with my proposition. What is her angle? This feels like some sort of test, perhaps even a planned move to watch me fail so she can walk away feeling superior and rub my blunder in my face.

I must turn this around on her. I will not let another infernal human get one over on me and make me look like a fool.

"You asked me to assemble a team, and I choose you," I say. "It will be you, me, and the south patrol. The others will spread out to make up the difference around the perimeter while we're gone."

The captain is a soldier, too, and she can't turn me down

and still save face. She would look like a coward sitting behind a desk.

Now if I fail, it's her failure, too.

She appears completely unfazed by my selection. "And that's your final decision? You want me to prove that I can put my coin where my mouth is?"

She's very blunt, I must admit. It reminds me of an orc. "I simply thought you would want to do the honors of catching the Black Fox yourself," I say.

I don't think she believes it for a moment, but she gives me a curt smile anyway. She has shining, flat white teeth underneath her soft, pink-brown lips, and I marvel for a second at her demure canines. Her petite, round face is almost beautiful when she smiles.

For a moment I see Nera's face, and my chest constricts. I quickly turn away.

"We'll depart at dawn tomorrow," the captain says behind me. I nod quickly, once, and stride out.

Have I made a mistake by bringing her along? Too late to course-correct now. I am an orc, sturdy and steadfast, and I won't change my mind.

Soon it's the early morning, and we're assembled in pairs to venture out into the desert in the direction the Black Fox was seen fleeing. I think I catch a mischievous glint in Captain Mastair's eye as we set off. I've paired us up together, of course. Then she'll be the first to witness it when I succeed.

We walk at a quick clip into the endless sands. Neither of us speaks once we leave the city behind. We're a human and a trollkin, after all. We have nothing to say to each other that wouldn't start an argument. The last thing I want is to be indicted again for not calling her *sir*.

The wind is starting to pick up, and we have a lot of ground to cover in one day without taking camels with us. I thought we should stay as inconspicuous as possible, just to better our chances of finding the slippery thief, and riding in on camels is a great way to give ourselves away. The captain has a compass to make sure we don't get lost.

I let her lead the way, walking just a few paces behind. Her dark hair is cropped close to her head so none of it gets in her eyes, which is practical for this environment. From this position I can well and truly get a good look at her wide hips, bound tightly by cloth pants that hang loose around her legs, much like the flowing sleeves of her shirt. After an hour of walking through the blazing desert, her outfit makes much more sense. While the breeze gently ruffles her clothing, likely bringing fresh air against her arms and legs, my tight leathers and mail are becoming claustrophobically hot. She walks with a powerful determination, each step through the shifting sand as certain as the one before it. This is a woman in charge who very well knows it.

A little gnawing sensation begins in the base of my spine as I watch her, and it only grows as we crest a dune and she stops to check the compass, then continues onward in silence. I'm mesmerized by the swaying of her hips, the way every step she takes makes her ass perfectly pronounced and outlined. The longer we walk, the more I want to take one cheek in my big hand and squeeze it.

I shove the thought back down into the dirt where it belongs. I despise this woman. Not only is she human—as if that weren't enough—but she's arrogant, and lacking in self-control, and she has the most appealing curve between her waist and her hip—

I groan. Why are humans such alluring creatures? Nera gave me a taste, and now it's like a disease has taken root in me.

I can't make that mistake again. I will never make that mistake again. It's wrong, immoral, to want a human the way I have.

Suddenly, the captain comes to an abrupt halt, and I stop next to her. She's staring down at the compass.

"This is odd." She holds it up, and instead of pointing a single direction as intended, the indicator is wobbling back and forth. "Magnetic activity," she says, turning her gaze out into the endless sand ahead of us. "It could mean a few different things."

"Are any of them dangerous?" I ask. The Hazrain is not my home, but the captain seems familiar enough with it—and she dresses the part, golden rings in her ears and all.

"There could be a storm somewhere out there," she says. "But nothing close by. Yet."

I don't point out that we haven't found any sign of the Black Fox, either. Maybe my plan was a foolhardy one, and there's a good chance she'll hold it against me after this. With the compass suddenly misbehaving, it should be time to turn around and start back the way we came, or return later with camels so we can travel farther.

Instead of any of these things, I say, "If we just continue straight, we won't need the compass."

As if I'd give up now and risk looking like a fool in front of her. Perhaps I sacrificed most of my pride in the Narzag-kig, but I still have a few shreds left.

No, we will push on.

ZIRELLE

I expected this to be some kind of ploy for the lieutenant to get me alone and interrogate me. I thought he would poke and prod me, trying to get under my skin and convince me to break through my mask. He doesn't like me, not one bit, so that's the only reason I can imagine for pairing us together.

Instead he walks silently behind me for hours, never once interrupting my thoughts. I grow bored after a while without any sort of conversation, not that I can admit that. So we walk and walk without speaking—until the compass starts acting up.

This unnerves me. While magnetic storms aren't uncommon in the Hazrain, they're not the sort of thing you want to get stuck in. If one were to sneak up on us out in the open like this and encase us in its vortex, we would not emerge alive. Only our bones would be left.

But Agkar wants us to continue, and I know why. This was his idea. If we don't find what we came for, he'll look like an idiot, and that's the last thing an arrogant orc like the lieutenant wants.

"Let's press on," he says, before quickly adding, "sir."

The way he looks right in my eyes as he insists on continuing forward, I think it must be a challenge, and I can't possibly turn that down. Life is just a series of challenges, one hurdle after another, that only those who work the hardest can overcome. I can't show any fear in front of this orc if I want him to respect me, and that's all I want of any of my subordinates. Hard work and respect.

Besides, the lieutenant was right when he suspected I wanted to catch the Black Fox myself. The bastard has been a symbol of my failure for most of my tenure as captain. Every time one of our merchants is robbed blind, it's a tarnish on my reputation in Attirex. When I go to bed at night, I think how I've failed the city by letting him get away with this.

If I brought the Black Fox back bound up in rope myself, I could finally shake off the dishonor like a dusty cloak. Maybe then my parents' ghosts would be proud.

"Fine," I say, rolling my shoulders back and setting my feet apart. "We'll continue."

Lieutenant Agkar nods, a smug look on his face. Insolent orc.

So we trek onward, occasionally glancing back to ensure our footprints are headed the right direction. Up in the distance, we catch sight of some great orange rocks, and I'm suddenly excited. No one would be foolish enough to set up camp right out here in the desert, naturally. But under the shelter of some cliffs? I could very well see the Black Fox hiding out here, his nest built into one of the many cave systems that run underneath the Hazrain.

Those infernal caves are the main reason that enforcing the law here is so difficult. You never know what criminal enterprise has taken up residence in the long-vacant burrows of the great worms—or what ancient ruin you might stumble into. Thank goodness the worms have gone extinct and only their bones remain, huge sculptures that occasionally dot the dunes. Now they have become the stuff of myths, like so many other magical legends of the desert.

This time Agkar does walk at my side. I'm not sure what's changed, but he keeps his eyes straight ahead as we trudge through the sand, and he remains as deadly silent as before. I wonder what the purpose of all this was? I was certain he had an agenda, some reason for inviting me out to tromp across the desert alone together, but it hasn't shown itself to me yet.

I try not to focus on the big trollkin lumbering along next to me, but now he's harder to ignore. When I'm finally tired of the tedium, I decide to go for the throat and see where the cracks appear. That's always been my style.

"Why did you come here, Lieutenant?" I ask, splintering the silence.

His head jerks up, surprised to find me speaking.

"Well," he says with a grunt, "I figure it's only fair that if I assign a mission, I also go on that mission."

A good answer, but not the one I was looking for. "To the Hazrain, I mean. You elected to transfer to the least hospitable place you could possibly go, did you not?"

A deep discomfort settles on his face. The question I've asked has disturbed something inside him, and I spot that uncanny, distant look in his eyes again. He doesn't answer my question, so in annoyance, I start walking faster.

After a moment, Agkar catches up. His voice is hard and gruff as he says, "I had to leave."

Oh, so he's going to talk to me after all.

"Why?" I ask. I'm genuinely curious what could've driven away a tough, stubborn orc like him. He hates humans, as most trollkin do—but even more so, as if it's something personal.

The lieutenant clams up again, mouth set in a tight line.

"Fine, fine." I wave a hand dismissively. "We don't have to get into it. But if you had to leave, why come here? No one does by choice."

"This was the only place I could go." His voice is tight. Perhaps we're a little too close to whatever he's hiding.

"Ah." I nod in understanding. "A last resort."

"I suppose."

I wonder if it was a love affair gone wrong. For some reason I don't have a hard time picturing this. I'm sure for orc and troll ladies, Agkar is a catch. If I were into seven-foot-tall men with olive skin, I would probably think he was attractive.

As soon as I think it, I want to un-think it. He's an orc, and there is no such thing as an attractive orc. Even if he is built like a house and fills out his uniform rather nicely. Even if he has arms as thick as fence posts and hands the size of dinner plates. Even if—

I rub my temple. This isn't doing me any good.

"Captain?" Agkar asks. I raise my head, dropping my hand to my side. "Do you need water? We should watch for heat stroke out here."

I laugh at the idea. Me, getting heat stroke in the desert? But his concern takes me by surprise.

"I'm all right. My body is adjusted to the heat. Thank you though, Lieutenant."

He just grunts in answer, and I think that's going to be the most I get from him. More minutes of silence pass until suddenly Agkar asks, "Why are you here... sir?" I didn't expect this to be a two-way conversation. "You speak Trollkin," he adds. "That makes me wonder how you ended up in this hole."

Aren't I just the human woman who goes around telling him what to do? He doesn't care who I am. Or he hasn't, before now.

I weigh what to say. I could admit that both of my parents were soldiers, too, and that's why I joined as soon as I could: To carry on their legacy, to honor them and do right by their memory. Besides, the service is the easiest way to make a living if you're sixteen and penniless.

That feels foolish, though. I'd be exposing my most vulnerable self to the lieutenant, something I'd probably regret.

Instead I say, "I'm here because I grew up here." I gesture around us. "I was born in Attirex, I've lived here all my life, and I imagine I will probably die here, too."

Chapter 3

Agkar

So she grew up under the canopies among both humans and trollkin. I didn't expect it, but it explains a lot about her.

"So you've only ever served here?" I ask. I can't help it. I'm curious about this woman who's always lived at the juncture of human and trollkin kind, and then managed to rise up the ranks to captain.

Know thy enemy.

"Yes, ever since I joined the military as a teenager," the captain says. So we've both been soldiers since the beginning. "There was never any reason for me to leave. This is my home."

I see—and I've insulted it a few times now. As inhospitable as the desert is, I know what it means to have a homeland and care for it in its own unique way. While my homeland may look like nothing but bare plains and dead, rocky crags to most, it is still home to me.

Perhaps I should be more careful with what I'm saying.

No. It's no concern of mine whether or not I hurt her feelings.

"But I didn't always speak your language," the Captain continues, adjusting her pack. "I've lived adjacent to it, then I learned more once I took this position."

"You are good at it," I say, without really thinking first. Then I correct myself. "Your grasp of the language is decent."

She snorts, and it is both more casual and less ladylike than I expected. "You can compliment me, Lieutenant. I won't take it personally."

I huff. I didn't intend to compliment her. For a moment, though, I'm embarrassed that I don't speak any Freysian at all when the captain has put so much effort into learning our tongue, and fluently. She's more dedicated to her work than I'd thought.

I don't speak further, and neither does she as we continue walking, but more questions are swirling inside me. What drove her to claw her way to the top? Why does she smell like alcohol every day? What is it she's trying to drink away? I shouldn't care about any of these things, but I'm drawn back over and over. The captain walks more stiffly beside me, as if she's also holding something locked up inside.

At last, we arrive at the base of the huge cliffs. The captain checks her compass again, and the indicator swings from side to side as we approach the towering orange rocks. They're all flat on one side and sloping down gently on the other, like the earth was shifted sideways in just this one spot.

"That's not good," she says, pocketing the compass. "Keep to the edge of the cliffs as we go."

She doesn't look to see if I've obeyed her command, and starts walking along the bare wall of rock as close to it as possible. As I follow along behind, the sheer cliff face feels endless. Then, suddenly, Captain Mastair stops in front of me, and I bump into her from behind. I feel every last inch of her backside against my front before I quickly step back. It sends a jolt of heat through me—but before I can say anything, the captain glances back and holds up a finger to her lips, then nods once.

She's found something.

It was only her firm ass against my legs, purely an accident, and yet every place her body touched mine is buzzing, thickening my blood.

The captain ducks her head down low as she looks around a corner I hadn't seen before. Whatever this is, it's disguised cleverly in the cliffside. She squints hard, then takes another step, suddenly disappearing into the rock. When I peer around the edge, I see her heading into a darkened crevasse. There's no light coming from within.

"The torch, lieutenant?" she whispers. I take off my pack and pull out a torch covered in cloth, then a fire-starter. Once the torch is lit, she takes it and we start off into the cave. I let her lead again. If there are any booby traps, she'll set them off first.

Oddly, my gut clenches at the thought.

There's not much to see here, and soon I'm convinced we've stumbled across a geological phenomenon and nothing else. Mountains are always riddled with odd ravines and caverns like this that ultimately lead nowhere. Still, sureness of the captain's steps and the powerful set of her shoulders keeps me quiet and following her lead.

As we head deeper, the cavern shrinks, and I figure this investigation will peter out on its own. Perhaps I lost my gambit here today, and we won't find the Black Fox. But the captain simply crouches down and continues, even as the tunnel grows more and more awkward. It's a bit more of a reach for me to get low enough, but I do, because I won't let my much greater size impede me from going where the captain goes.

Then, up ahead, the light of the torch reflects off of a rock face. It's far away, but it looks like this cavern comes to an end.

"Lieutenant," Captain Mastair whispers as she comes to a sudden halt in front of me. I almost bump into her again. "I think we've found him."

ZIRELLE

I had a feeling there was something hidden inside this cliff, and sure enough, here it is.

There's no other light inside, so I assume the occupants are out for now. This is good—whoever is hiding out here will not be expecting company when they return.

When we enter the cavern I find the ceiling is far higher than I expected, and it sprawls a long way across. There's enough space in here to house a hundred people, and it is most certainly in use.

It's been arranged in a practical manner, with a fire pit close to the exit to allow the smoke out, and five bedrolls arranged around it in a circle. Tapestries hang from the walls, and there's writing etched into the stone here and there—tally marks, numbers, and names I don't know. On the far end of the cavern is a pile of goods, surely all stolen.

I know this belongs to the Black Fox because he has a poster of himself by the fire pit. I pick it up and show it to Agkar. "Got him."

I have to admit that the lieutenant was right. We found our guy out here in the desert. Now that we know where he's hiding, we just have to leave no trace of ourselves and watch from a distance until he returns. Then we'll spring our trap.

To my surprise, though, Agkar doesn't gloat. "We had better leave quickly," he says, his tenor serious and urgent. "They could be back at any time. We should return with backup."

Right. The lieutenant is being pragmatic. We don't have time to savor this victory. The Black Fox is more than just one person, as indicated by the bedrolls. We have a small gang on our hands and we'll need a larger force to handle them.

I leave the poster where I found it and head back to the low tunnel that will lead us out of the cavern, holding the torch in front of me. It's awkward, but our way grows easier the closer we get to the exit.

That's when I hear it—*whoosh*ing. Up ahead the air is bright orange with blowing sand. It makes a monstrous whistling sound as it blows past the cavern entrance.

A sand storm.

I stop abruptly, and Agkar bumps into me again. "You need to speak up when you're going to do that," he grunts.

I don't answer. I pull out the compass again even though I know what it will say already.

Sure enough, the indicator is spinning in circles.

"A magnetic storm," I tell him, bile rising in my throat. "We're trapped."

Agkar

I should have paid closer attention when the captain expressed concern about the compass. But no, I was just too eager to be right and prove it, and now we're stuck here until the sandstorm passes.

I hate this forsaken desert.

"How long will it take to blow over?" I ask as we return to the main cavern. At least we know the Black Fox won't be able to return in the meantime, either.

"Unknown," Captain Mastair says. "Could be anywhere from a few hours to a few days."

My mind goes blank. "Days?" She can't mean that.

"It depends on how big the storm is." She attempts to keep her expression firm and impassive, as her soldier's training demands, but I don't miss the clench of her hand into a fist at her side.

I sit down heavily on the floor of the cavern. We could be stuck here for days, just the two of us, in this isolated little cave. It is a deeply horrifying thought to be confined to such a tight space together for who knows how long. I know she loathes me as much as I loathe her, as hard as she tries to keep it locked behind her stern face. Will we tear each other apart?

When I think of her taut, round ass, a very different fear crawls into my mind. It won't just be her commands grating on my nerves. I'm going to have to get this lust under control, too. I can't make that mistake again.

"We could brave the storm," I say. "Cover our heads with our packs."

The captain stares at me like I've grown an extra set of arms, then her eyebrows tilt like she pities me. "Have you been in a Hazrainian sandstorm before, Lieutenant?"

"Of course not. I'm from a more civilized part of the world."

The captain scowls at my jab. "Then you have no idea what you're talking about. Unless we had a full body of heavy leathers and helmets and goggles, there's no way of braving a sandstorm. It would flay the skin off your bones." She shakes her head at me like I'm a foolish child. "Unless you're into that kind of thing."

I can't help the shiver that ripples up my arms. I'd rather not get lacerated to a skeleton by sand. It's a slightly worse outcome than being trapped for days with only Captain Mastair for company, stuck in this cave with the person I detest most in the world, and who has the most incredible rear end I've ever seen.

I've got to stop this.

While I'm caught up in my thoughts, the captain picks through the Black Fox's belongings.

"Won't they know we were here if we disturb their things?" I ask. When they return, our surprise attack will no longer be much of a surprise. They could even panic and flee before we can catch them.

"We won't survive otherwise." The captain just shrugs as she pulls a water skin from a bag and drinks from it. "We'll just have to come up with a new plan. I imagine they'll return as soon as the storm clears."

Oh. I understand now. "And we'll be here," I say. "Prepared for them."

"Precisely."

Except that could be days away, and there's only the two of us versus five of them. We would have to truly get the element of surprise for this to work. But if anyone can pull it off, it would be the captain. I know after the Hookclaws that she has the tactical experience.

"Ah!" Captain Mastair holds up two big sacks, pleased. "Food. Lots of it. We should have enough supplies here to get by for a while at least."

What could she mean by *a while*? I grunt in annoyance. "I thought you said it would be a day or two at most."

"There's no way to know with a sandstorm. There have been stories of sandstorms in certain parts of the desert that lasted for a week. Sometimes multiple weeks."

These are not the words I want to be hearing right now. A few days sounded bad, but I could bear the idea. Weeks, though? We would not emerge alive after chewing each other's heads off, not to mention the lack of proper supplies.

The captain is keeping her cool, though, so I will, too. Instead I try to think of what needs to be done immediately. If I can keep my mind on the here and now, I won't be able to dread how long we'll be stuck here.

Captain Mastair busies herself with rifling through all of the Black Fox's packs, pulling out things that could be useful and making a big pile. She doesn't kneel down or crouch as she does it, but bends over at the hip so her butt with the tight cloth pants sticks straight up into the air. It feels like some kind of taunt, but I know it's not directed at me. She doesn't think twice about my existence as she continues working, and I decide to make myself useful as well.

I have many questions: Where will we bathe? Go to the bathroom? I wander to the farthest end of the cave, and to my surprise there's a smaller cavern nestled low to the ground, filled with water—clear, beautiful water.

"Oh, good!" the captain exclaims from across the cave. "I found more fuel. I was worried the torch would go out."

I'm relieved by this, too. Sitting in the darkness with just Captain Mastair for company? I would regretfully decline.

As for bowel movements, there are some chamber pots in one far corner, and they reek. Disgusting. I take a piss in one anyway because we don't have a lot of options, and I don't want to pollute our fresh water supply.

I make my way back to where the captain is seated on the floor, lording over her spoils. She's rather bright-eyed when I return, and I don't understand how she could be this optimistic while we face being trapped here together for—

Don't think about it.

"They have everything," she says with wonder. "Water, food, wood. As far as places to get stranded, this is about as good as it gets."

"There's fresh water, too." I point to the other end of the cave. "Plenty for drinking and bathing."

Her eyes jump up to mine at this last word, and she tilts her head. "Why do you care about that?"

It takes me a few moments to realize that I should be insulted by this question. "Do you think trollkin don't bathe?" I ask, incredulous.

The captain looks surprised by my response. "I just assumed it wasn't high on the priority list."

I cross my arms and grunt. Humans really think their shit smells like daisies. "We wash ourselves just as much as humans do. Maybe even more. A clean body is a clean mind."

"Hmm." She doesn't say anything else. Then she stands up and searches the edges of the cave for something, returning a few minutes later with an armful of wood and some tinder. Neither of us speaks as she builds a little tent with her supplies. Clearly the captain knows how to start a fire.

Eventually she says, "Sorry." She's not looking at me as she takes a fire starter out of her pack. "That was kind of an asshole thing for me to say."

At first, I'm not sure if I'm hearing her right. Is she apologizing for her comment about bathing? I'm so flabbergasted that I don't answer immediately.

"I will try not to be offended," I say at last. "There's a lot we don't understand about each other." As much as it sets my teeth on edge, perhaps I should play the diplomat this time, or else we won't survive this.

The captain turns to face the fire as the smoke blows out the entrance of the cave. "Isn't it strange?" she says. "One of the few places in the world we have to get along."

"We don't have to get along to do our jobs." My tone is firm. "We just have to do them."

She's silent for a long moment, poking the fire with a stick.

"Right," the captain says, and that's all. She keeps her face turned away so I can't see her expression, and I wonder what she was expecting me to say. I'm trollkin; she's human. Anywhere else in the world and we'd be trying to kill each other.

Unfortunately, I cannot stop thinking about that ass of hers high up in the air as she bent over the supplies, or tensing and releasing as she walked through the heavy sand. The longer I'm in close quarters with her, the more I find myself staring. Studying her. Building a little mental image of her that I can look at whenever I want.

It's that mental image I bring to mind as we lie in our separate bedrolls that night as far from each other as possible, the fire burning down to smoldering ashes between us. Captain Mastair's eyes are small but dark, nearly black, and she has eyelashes so long she could sweep a floor with them. Her shape is extravagant, winnowing from broad shoulders to a slight waist, and then back out again into thick hips and thighs. Unbidden, I imagine those thighs squeezing around my head. They would be fiercely strong, I know, yet soft at the same time.

No. Absolutely not. I don't need to be thinking of my superior officer this way—especially not my human superior officer. My heart is already beating faster, though, and I can't seem to stop it. I've been between an orcess's legs before, of course. During those rare times of peace, women seek us out, and in the past I've taken the opportunity. But that was a matter of sating my base urges and keeping my needs in check. The only time I've felt lust like what I'm feeling now...

I can't go there. I must be getting cabin fever already. I try to breathe deeply and fall asleep, but unfortunately, I've developed a raging hard-on. The bedroll covers are too thick to make it obvious, but I turn away from the captain anyway so I can't even make out the shape of her shoulders or hips under her blankets.

I must have managed to pass out because that night, I dream about walking behind Captain Mastair up dune after dune of sand, never taking my eyes off of her. I want nothing more than to reach out and touch her, and so in the dream, I do. She gasps with surprise at first, but then sinks backwards into me, my cock pressed up against the crease between those delightful round cheeks. Her body gives to me as I take it firmly in my hands, savoring every last inch of her.

When I wake up sweaty and tense from my wet dreams, the cavern is dark, merely a smidgen of light coming in through the crack in the cave entrance. The fire is out. In the pitch blackness I can't tell if I'm the only one up or not, so I quietly say, "Captain?"

There's a muffled groan, and I think I must have woken her. I root around for the torch and pull out my fire-starter. The captain rubs her face in a very unladylike way, and I enjoy watching while she shakes off sleep. She's far less tense now than she is during the day, her body lithe and relaxed. There's a vulnerability to her that I've never seen before, an honesty in the way she moves and breathes, as if she isn't carefully curating herself for once.

Then I head to the end of the tunnel to see if anything has changed with the storm outside, but it's still nothing but a slate of orange sand rushing past, howling like a banshee.

We're trapped.

Chapter 4

Zirelle

"**D**amn it," Agkar curses as he returns from checking on the storm. I dig through the food supplies, trying to decide what to eat. I settle on some dried apricots and sit down on my bedroll.

Neither of us speaks that morning. Confined to such a small space together, the air is tense, and this is just the first morning of who knows how many.

This time Agkar is the one who gets the fire lit, as he should. I watch with interest as he piles up the fuel and builds a little pyramid with wood around it. He's taken off the outer layer of his uniform, leaving only a lightweight jerkin that goes to the tips of his shoulders. I like the way his muscles ripple as he leans forward to bring the flame to the tinder, biceps flexing as he performs each task in silence. He's pretty ripped, I have to admit. There are muscles in his back I've never even seen on a human before. He's pure strength, just tinted olive green.

Having these thoughts about a trollkin is disgusting.

They've murdered my kind, razed our cities, stolen our land. But onward my imagination goes anyway, drawing my attention again and again to his dense, strong body.

Agkar looks up and catches me watching. Instead of turning away, I simply continue to stare. You have to remember that when you're the boss, especially the boss of trollkin, you must never look away. Everything you do, even if wrong, should seem intentional and measured.

Agkar just rolls his eyes and returns to what he's doing. Soon the fire is going and the cave starts to warm up. I didn't realize how cold I was until just now. With the flames picking up speed, we put out the torch to save our stores. The fire eats fuel, too, so we'll have to be careful about how we use it to avoid clearing out all of the Black Fox's stores.

Neither of us has said a word, so I decide I should find something to do. First I check out the pile of goods on one end of the cavern. I'm not ready to think about bathing yet, not with Agkar here, though I probably should after yesterday's march. I examine everything the Black Fox has taken—jewels, gold candelabras, weapons, even some random objects like glass bottles and books. I take a dagger and slip it into my belt, then retrieve another bigger one. When I return to the fire, Agkar doesn't look up.

"Here." I extend the large dagger, handle facing him. "You should take this." Squinting suspiciously at me, he doesn't accept my offering, so I add in a lower voice, "Lieutenant."

His natural frown deepens into a scowl, pulling his curved tusks downward. But he understands that it's a command, so he snatches the dagger from my hand, much too quickly.

The point tilts and slices across my palm, and I hiss under my breath as it breaks through the skin. Agkar gives me a strange look as I pull my hand back, clenching my palm in my fist. I don't want him to see me bleed. But the droplets fall to the floor anyway, and his eyes dart toward them. He scrunches up his face.

"It cut you." The lieutenant lets out a snarl. "Stupid. You must have been holding the blade wrong."

"No, you grabbed it wrong. You were too busy being pissy with me."

"Pissy?!" His green-gold eyes spark.

"Yes, pissy. Look, I'm not asking to be best friends." I sit back down on the other side of the fire to examine my wound. "I just want to tolerate each other." Because if we can do that, this will all go by much faster.

The orc growls but doesn't snap back. Then, after a few moments, he sighs and gestures at me. "Let me look at it."

"Huh?"

"Your hand. Bring it over here."

I keep it at my side. "It's fine. Just a scratch." I can tell I'm really irritating him now.

"This place is filthy. If your wound is dirty, it could get infected, and that would be a much more serious problem." Agkar grabs my wrist. I try to pull it away, but his grip is firm. "Don't be a baby."

Annoyed but cowed, I stay still as Agkar reaches into his pack and pulls out a small bag. He removes a few objects carefully: a bottle of cleaning solution, some bandages, and a needle and thread. I did not expect a big, beefy orc who's used to being in charge to carry around a med kit—and a homemade one, at that.

He cleans the wound first, and he's surprisingly gentle. His fingers are huge in comparison to my arm, and he only has four of them, but they work just as effectively as my five do. It stings, of course, but I don't let any discomfort show on my face. I see his eyes flick up and then back down again as he swaps out the fluid for some salve in a small jar.

"Where did you get all this?" I ask. "It isn't military issue."

"No." His hands slow down as he applies the salve using just his fingers. I'm shocked at how delicate they are with me while being so large and calloused. "It's not."

He doesn't say any more as he works, but I have a gnawing feeling that this is connected, whatever it is, to why he's here. Suddenly I want to know that secret, more than anything.

"How did you learn this, Lieutenant?" I ask him. "We're not usually trained in first aid."

Agkar jabs at me a little harder as he puts on the salve, then drops my hand. "Someone taught me."

"Is that someone the reason you left your post?" I ask.

His eyes are hardened daggers when he looks back up at me.

"Lieutenant?" I press.

"Are you asking me to tell you as my captain?" he asks, his voice dangerously low. "Or as Zirelle?"

The way he says my name in his low, grumbling voice is... delicious.

Of course my question is coming from me as me. But if he's so intent on holding rank, then I'll treat him like such. "Sir," I remind him.

He grunts angrily and looks away. I feel like he probably wants to claw my face off.

"I should know who's working under me," I say. "If something drove you away from your post, what's not to say the same won't happen here and leave us high and dry again?"

Agkar tenses up, then turns his head so he's facing the fire. "It was a woman," he says. "A human woman. She's the reason I left."

AGKAR

Why is she dragging this out of me? Captain Mastair—no, Zirelle, that's her name—is intent on making me tell her my sordid, ugly history. Which, as it turns out, concerns a human woman.

As she also is. This will certainly not go well.

Her bright eyes are wide as she considers my words. "Wow." She strokes her chin thoughtfully. "That's not what I expected."

I just want to get up and storm out of this forsaken cave. She can't keep me here, can she? Not if I decide to just go out and brave the skin-flaying sandstorm.

"So, a human woman drove you off," the captain repeats. Before I can stop it, I turn to her and snarl loudly—loud enough to certainly count as insubordination. Suddenly I don't care anymore. What's she going to do here to punish me?

"It's none of your business," I hiss.

But Zirelle isn't put off, not in the least. In fact, she leans towards me, clearly unafraid. A human woman who isn't afraid of *me*? I could kill her in a split second, just snap her in half, but it's like the thought has never occurred to her.

There's wonder in her voice as she says, "Is that why you're so testy and insubordinate toward me all the time? Because of her?"

I'm flabbergasted. How can she brush it off so easily and then make it about herself? "No," I growl. This dredging up of my past is making me angry. "I'm insubordinate because I hate that I have to stand there and let you tell me what to do!" My voice comes out a bellow.

Even then... the captain doesn't back off. She must have a death wish.

"Why?" she asks, her eyes wide. "You've had commanding

officers before. Your former superior sent you here with glowing recommendations. Surely you know how to follow orders."

I clench my hand into a fist because otherwise I might do something I regret. "I only take orders from those who deserve my respect."

There's a slight twitch in her eye that stands out from her otherwise calm, unflappable demeanor. I've made a dent, but she won't show it.

"So you think I don't deserve your respect." Zirelle sits back, crossing her feet in front of her like this isn't the tensest moment between us since I arrived in Attirex.

What reason do I have to respect a human? Especially one as irritating and demanding as her? She's weak and small—inferior in every way.

"Why?" she asks again, even more persistent. "What have I done that makes it impossible for you to treat me the way I deserve? Human or not, I'm your superior. It's your job to listen to me."

I'm done with this conversation. As if I need to justify myself, but I'll do it anyhow.

"You ride my ass and everyone else's," I snarl. "You demand everything be done a certain way. You are, frankly, a fucking pain. And you stink of alcohol every day." I take a deep breath, having spewed that out all at once. "I can't respect a superior officer who succumbs to the drink."

Zirelle's face, at last, gives away her true feelings. Her eyes are wide and her eyebrows are drawn, like I've fully taken her off-guard. I might even detect a trace of hurt, which surprises me. I didn't think Captain Mastair had a single hole in her thick armor.

She looks down at her hand and the bandage I've wound around it, and her voice is calm as she says, "I see." But that hand is trembling a little. "I work hard every day, as hard as I possibly can, and it's still never enough." She squeezes her fist tight, which must hurt with the fresh wound on her palm. "It will never be enough, will it? Even if I worked myself to death, it wouldn't be enough for you."

I don't know what to say. She does stay late every night, finishing paperwork. She never takes a meal or break. She's always going somewhere or doing something important without a falter in her step.

Maybe it wears on her.

Before I can reply, she stands up, hands clenched tight at her sides, and walks away to do something by the fresh water. There's a coolness, a tightness to her back, as she takes stock of it.

I should be glad to be rid of her, but I find that I don't feel good about what I've said.

For most of the day I stay on the other end of the cavern, picking through stolen goods. For a lack of anything better to do, I sort them in a way that might help us return them later. What a good lawman I am now, I think. From a lieutenant on the front lines of the war, to sleeping in a cave with my human superior and deciding which petty merchant will get their livelihood back.

Off on the other end of the cave, I hear a breathy exhale echo throughout the cavern. When I turn around, I catch Zirelle's backside as she slides into the water.

It's like a lamp being lit, and instantly I'm as thick and hard as a log. I can't help but stare as she slides all the way into the water and lets out a satisfied moan. My pulse is throbbing inside me and my cock is pulling hard at my pants. Damn it all —I'm just in my trousers and left the coil that wraps around my waist where I slept last night. I can't even stand up or risk her seeing just how alert she's made me.

All it took was that little slip of back and a peek of side, and now I'm desperate to be in that water with her. I would seize her around the waist and pull her body flush against mine, so she could feel my cock pressing at her beautiful ass. The urge to fuck her fast and hard descends on me like a swarm of flies. I turn my head slightly back towards the pool, where Zirelle now floats to and fro silently. I can only make out the curve of her neck and her curly hair above the surface of the water, but I'm so swollen I can't even remember what I'm supposed to be doing.

Fuck. I want her, badly, and that's the worst thing that could possibly happen.

CHAPTER 5

ZIRELLE

If we're going to avoid each other, perhaps this is the best time for me to finally bathe. If he has no respect for me, neither do I have any respect for him. He's an orc, after all. A brute. How could I have expected anything different? That was my mistake. Of course it doesn't matter to the lieutenant how hard I try to be a good captain, to do my job well, and make sure the city stays safe. None of that makes a difference to a trollkin when there's a line gouged in the sand between us. There's nothing I can do to earn his loyalty.

I take off my clothes and slide into the water, expecting it to be brutal cold. Instead it's mild, even pleasant. Agkar stays put where he is, crouched like a goblin over the Black Fox's loot pile.

Why does it upset me so much that the lieutenant seems to... well, hate me? I'm a human woman working in the Attirex guard—the approval of others hasn't meant much to me over the course of my life. I got to where I am by disregarding what anyone thinks about me and my capabilities, and pushing on towards what I want. When I was promoted to captain over Corporal Jar'kel, he resented me for almost a year. To this day I still detect envy and irritation when I ask him to do a task.

At least the corporal knows his place now, and does his job without disrespecting me to my face. Agkar's disapproval hurts deeper. He's intelligent, capable, and could be a good soldier if only we had a decent working relationship. I want him to see me as worthy of his obedience.

An uncomfortable thought settles on me. I've been ruminating far too often about how he looks, what a marvelous body he has, how the stiff line of his mouth is just begging to be cracked into a grin. I couldn't imagine what that looks like, but I want to. Completely unbidden, the thought of the lieutenant without that sleeveless jerkin crawls into my mind's eye. He's been forged with steel from training his body all his life, just like I have. He has a sharp mind, that much is clear to me.

And he has very gentle hands.

I duck my head under the surface of the water, letting it swallow me up. I have to banish these thoughts and bury them deep down, where they belong. I cannot be thinking of an orc this way. It's not just disgusting to me, personally, but I would be ostracized if anyone found out. There are lines one simply doesn't cross. Perhaps a mere citizen could dabble, but not me.

Instead of ruminating over what could never happen between us, I decide to investigate this curious spring that flows with fresh water. Where the cavern wall ends, the pool underneath continues on into a dark tunnel, and I wonder where it goes.

There's no booze among the Black Fox's stores. That was a tough realization. It's the vent I use for my frustration, a salve for all the tasks that lay undone every night. Now there are more and more of them piling up on my desk while we remain here trapped in the sandstorm, problems that no one else will solve. I need some kind of outlet or I'm going to explode, and surely the lieutenant will get caught in the fallout. I can't break like that in front of him, not now. I need another way to release this terrible energy inside me. If I can't drink, maybe a bodily release is what's called for.

I duck inside the tunnel, where perhaps I can find somewhere a little more... private. There are a few inches of air between the surface of the water and the ceiling, just enough for me to keep my head above water. This narrow cavern is also oddly straight, as if it was carved this way rather than worn in by time. I wonder if the Black Fox did this, or if it was someone who was here before them. So I swim on, wondering what I might find.

After a few moments of swimming, I catch sight of light scattering across the surface of the water. But it's not natural sunlight—it's *purple*. What could that possibly be?

As I paddle towards it, the ceiling gives way to a small cavern. It is obviously carved into the stone, made by artificial means. What's most surprising, though, are the runes on the far wall. It would be pitch black in here if it weren't for the glowing light emanating from the markings.

What am I looking at? What could this possibly be?

I climb out of the water, shivering a little because of my nakedness, and a little because I'm afraid of such a strange, otherworldly thing. Looking at the whole wall now, it's unmistakable: Two faces are etched into the stone, each line filled with that bright purple substance. One of the faces is clearly human, and the other has curved tusks, like a trollkin.

Maybe I should swim back to get Agkar and show him what I've found. I've never seen anything like this before, though I've heard rumors of old ruins hidden underneath the desert, buried by the sands of time. It's said there's ancient magic there, a relic of an era long past when humans and trollkin alike could wield it.

This is an incredible discovery.

For some reason, though, I stay put. Something about this feels private, like it was meant only for me. This strange depiction on the wall of the two faces, looking into one another's eyes, means something. They are so close together, it's as if they're about to kiss.

Whatever this feeling is, I know it's why I'm finding it so difficult to let go of Agkar's opinion of me. I'm frustrated and enraged by the fact I'll never earn his respect, no matter how hard I try, because I want more than just respect. I think that I even want that big body on top of mine. I want to touch those thick arms and feel those huge, four-fingered hands encircle me. I want to know what his generous lips might taste like.

Oh, and there's more. There's so much more and I have to clench my eyes closed against it.

Though most of the time I rely on the drink to get me from day to day, sometimes I use a man's body to make me forget, too. But to want an orc is beyond the pale, even for me. It might even cost me my job.

Except I do want him, badly, and it's like an ache right at the juncture of my thighs. If it were Lieutenant Agkar climbing into the cool water with me, nothing left to hide his body... Instead of stopping my thoughts in their tracks, I let the fantasy play out this time. I imagine the lieutenant without his shirt on, crouching over me, one tusk pulling up the side of his mouth with a sultry smirk, the same way it does when he's being defiant. I've seen his package clearly outlined in his pants after he took off all that heavy mail, so I know he has something to work with down there.

I can't be thinking of him this way, entertaining filthy

thoughts about my subordinate officer. Except that imagining him is all I want to do in this strange, beautiful place that I've found, with this eerie light casting my skin in a purple glow.

Leaning back in the water, my hands trail down between my legs. I imagine it's Agkar's hand as I reach down and seek out the delicate bud there, where my folds are already swollen and warm. As my hand works, flicking my clit from side to side, I close my eyes and let my mind drift. I don't need to be ashamed of my own thoughts when no one can hear them but me. I visualize his expression, firmly determined as he pushes me down to the floor. He unlaces his pants, and what emerges from them thrills me. He would be so big and thick, and he would grunt as his big cock tested my tight wetness. I imagine it fitting inside me, filling me up, his breaths coming faster and harsher as he starts to move inside me.

It's not long before my legs are spasming and my pussy is clenching tight, wishing there was something in there to clench. My climax races from my hips up to my skull, and I groan as I lean back against the stone.

"Captain?" Lieutenant Agkar's voice echoes down the tunnel, and I freeze with my hand still between my thighs. There's a slightly worried edge to his voice.

"What is it, Lieutenant?" I call back. I'm ashamed and still aroused, so it comes out breathy and irritated.

"Hmph. Just wanted to make sure you hadn't been washed away." He grunts, and then I hear his heavy footsteps retreating.

When I'm finished, I sweep the little cavern with my eyes one last time, wondering what it means. Was this some sort of place of worship? I run my finger along the carving of the trollkin profile facing the human one. It's likely a mystery that I will never solve, but it's stirred something in me, a new idea I can't shake. Is it possible there was once something more between our civilizations?

Eventually, I swim down the tunnel toward the main cavern. When I surface, Agkar is sitting on the opposite end of the cave, and I can't tell what he's doing with his back facing me. This is the perfect time to get out of the water.

It's only once I'm out that I realize I'm soaking wet, with nothing I can use to dry myself. Padding across the bare cave floor toward one of the other bedrolls, I pick up a blanket and wick the water off of me. It's freezing in this cave, and I need to get my clothes back on so I can stir up the fire.

In my peripheral vision I catch Agkar turn slightly, checking that I'm there, and then quickly turn back around again when he sees that I'm still naked. He's likely gotten a good eyeful, and my blood heats at the idea.

I wonder what he's thinking. Not that I'll ever know. If I've gathered anything about the lieutenant, it's that he buries everything he feels deep down, and defends the walls with swords, arrows, and flaming pitch.

Eventually I put my base layer of clothes back on and add a single log to the fire. I'm freezing now that the water is evaporating off my skin, but I clench my teeth hard and hold the shivers in.

"Just put a blanket on," Agkar grumbles at me as he approaches the fire.

"I'm not cold."

"Yes, you are. Pathetic little human." His tone is dismissive, but then he picks up one of the blankets nearby and deposits it unceremoniously on my shoulders. "There's no point in playing tough."

"I'm not." I huff. "You must think pretty highly of yourself if you believe I'm putting on an air for you."

"Isn't that what you always do?" he asks. "Put on a mask so we'll be afraid of you?"

I'm so taken aback by this insight that I have no words at first. Agkar crouches down in front of the fire only a few feet away from me. Why isn't he over on the opposite side, the way he likes it?

"As if I'd spare a thought for what an orc thinks," I scoff. But he just looks into the flame, as if concentrating very hard. The silence stretches on, the atmosphere between us heavy and thick.

Finally, he says, "You do your job well, Captain."

I manage to stop my surprise from showing on my face just in time. Why is he complimenting me? It's more mysterious and impossible than the glowing cave markings I found.

And it makes me uneasy.

"I know I do," I say, even though that's a lie. I live in fear that soon someone will see through me and determine I don't deserve what I've built, but I must remain certain and sure to the lieutenant's face.

He just nods in response. "It has been difficult to accept the way things are here in Attirex, in the city guard," he says. "My only interaction with humans has been in the war or in servitude. Nothing prepared me for working alongside you—or cooperating with you."

"Servitude?" I ask.

"The human woman." He keeps his eyes firmly on the fire, as if he can't look at me as he says it. "She was my slave."

Right. The war. The trollkin probably still have plenty of human slaves in the cities they captured and burned to the ground. Well, the humans they didn't kill, anyway.

He does have a point. It's strange and unnatural to work side-by-side here while our people destroy each other. But the war has never touched us here, not beyond the news we receive. I've only ever lived in a world where we co-exist.

I pull some smoked meat out of the food stores and eat a piece. "But she's not yours anymore, I'm guessing." It's strange to be discussing a human woman that Lieutenant Agkar kept as a piece of property. Disturbing, if I'm honest—but I'm oddly pleased he's being open with me at last.

"No, she is not mine," he says. "I lost her in a Narzag-kig."

I take a bite. "What's that?"

"It's a fight to the death. Her mate, another orc, wanted her back from me. So I challenged him to a Narzag-kig, and he won." His shoulders curl and tighten, as if he very much wishes to forget that moment.

So Agkar went as far as to put his life on the line for this woman? "But you're still alive," I point out.

"Yes, unfortunately." He takes a deep breath, steeling himself for the rest of the story. "She saved me, petitioned for me not to lose my life, and I was disgraced. Dishonor on top of loss."

Oh. It's all starting to make a lot more sense now. She ran off with another orc and left the lieutenant licking his wounds. Surely he was crushed by this, if he cared about her the way I'm getting the sense that he did.

"I'm sorry," I say. "That sounds painful. It's no wonder you had to leave."

Agkar looks up at me, eyes slightly wide. Then he scowls. "You aren't gloating."

Does he see me as so vindictive? "No," I say, somewhat insulted. "Why would I? I've had my heart broken, too."

He doesn't answer at first, simply studying me like he's searching for something. Those bright eyes of his have a shocking depth to them, and I wonder just how much emotion he keeps buried down inside.

At last, Agkar asks me, "Who broke your heart?"

I know I'm the one who left this door open for him, but I'm surprised to find him stepping through it. He's fiddling with one of his tusks in what appears to be a nervous gesture.

It's a painful question to answer, but I asked him painful questions, too. Perhaps this is tit-for-tat.

"My parents," I say. "They were both soldiers." I rub my hands together, hoping the motion will help keep the tears out of my eyes. Just thinking about them, to this day, makes me crumble. "I didn't see them a lot growing up. When I was a teenager, they went on a routine patrol together. They must have come across someone who had a grudge against the city guard. Their bodies were found brutally beaten, their throats slashed, so both of them bled out before they died."

Agkar's face twists with an emotion I don't recognize. Shock? Horror?

"Is that the reason you became a soldier yourself?" he asks. "Revenge?"

Why does he suddenly want to know so much about me? His face is genuinely open, though, and he appears curious about my answer. For the first time, his guard isn't up, and how much I *like* it makes my chest clench.

I haven't spoken of my parents in many years, and I wonder what the cost of revealing my most secret pain to him might be. They are the weak link in my armor.

But I suppose there's no reward without risk.

"It's what I thought they would've wanted," I say. "For me to join the guard, too, and carry on their work. I want a better future for this city." Already my voice is wavering. What if he takes what I'm giving him and uses it as a cudgel against me later? Agkar is still listening, though, so I push through. "If they were here... I hope they'd be proud of me."

This is what drives me—what haunts me—every day of my

life. I want them looking down on me, pleased with what I've done, proud that I've risen to captain so I can better serve the people of Attirex.

"Is that why you drink so much?" Agkar asks. "Why you have a flask in your drawer? To forget?"

I'm flooded with humiliation.

"I don't know." It comes out tense and strained. "Maybe." I don't have a sufficient answer to explain my secret. I only hope that the lieutenant won't spill it to the other officers. I would surely struggle to hold onto my authority then.

"I won't tell anyone," he says after a moment, and there's a solemnity to it. "But you ought to restrain yourself. It will lead to a shorter life. I rely on you to do your job, and the drink might get in the way."

I grimace. He's hitting me right where it hurts.

"That's a lie," I snap. My embarrassment is twisting into anger. I need to defend myself. "You don't care anything for cooperation between us."

He seems surprised by my accusation. "I do insofar as I'm forced to."

Why are we both always on opposite sides of the same problem? I wish this could be different, that we could actually speak to each other without this thick veneer between us. I can't help but think back to the image in the cavern of the two faces, so close to one another. Why do I feel like it's asking something of me? Is it suggesting another, better way of existing?

I'm tired of looking away from this problem. I'm going to stare right into it, instead.

"We don't have to see each other as enemies, Agkar." His lips have just slightly parted at my use of his name, no rank attached. "I know that we're both soldiers. We've been trained to fight each other, not cooperate. But there are other options for humans and trollkin. You know there are, too. You've lived it already."

I hope that it does not set him off to bring up his heartbreak.

"I don't know what you mean." His expression is hard, but there is something else in his eyes that says perhaps, I'm not alone in how I feel.

"The human woman," I say. "She wasn't just your slave, was she?" I scoot just a little closer to him, close enough to feel the warmth of his body.

His breath hitches, and then he shakes his head. "No." It's barely more than a low growl. "She was... much more."

I nod. As I suspected. Does that mean he would go there again?

"Agkar," I begin, unsure what door I'm opening or how he'll respond to it. My voice drops almost to a whisper, as if saying it more quietly might save me from whatever consequences my question brings. "Was it just that woman? Or... could you see another human that way, too?"

Chapter 6

Agkar

I can't control the way my mouth falls open. Where my answer should be, there's a huge blank in my mind because of course I could, if that woman were *her*. My body is responding of its own accord to the captain's insinuation, my cock rising up eagerly in my trousers. I can't help but look at her small face, open to me and waiting for an answer. It's soft and heart-shaped, with a rounded nose and lips that look like they could belong many places quite comfortably. Her eyes are curious but shy in a way I could have never imagined, and I'm not sure I can bear it.

"It is not my place to even consider it, Captain," I say, trying to inject it with a force I don't feel. "It's inappropriate."

"Let's just pretend for a moment that you're not my lieutenant." She peers at me. "Can you?"

It's impossible. It's who I am. I might not care for her authority over me, but I will not let another human woman cut me open and spill out my innards like Nera did.

"No," I answer harshly. "I will not pretend." The captain leans back, surprised at my volume. I stand up and withdraw from the fire, because all I want to do is reach out and grab her. I want to tear open her clothes so I can see everything I missed while she climbed into the water earlier. I want to lick her between the legs until they're as far apart as they can get, and then wrap those legs around my hips and drive myself into her as deep as I can. I would watch as my cock sank inside her small, quivering hole, and keep fucking her until her tits were bouncing and she was crying out my name.

So I leave the fire behind and find a place to sit on the opposite end of the cave, as far from her as I can possibly get, because otherwise I would ravage her.

I cannot act on this. It would be against everything I've worked for, everything I've trained for. I've *killed* humans—dozens, maybe hundreds of them. I would be betraying the Grand Chieftain, my fellow trollkin, and myself. It's enough that my men in Gagzen witnessed the Narzag-kig and my pathetic attempt to keep Nera. I will not ruin my reputation in Attirex by bedding a human.

The captain doesn't speak to me again that night, and an unsettling silence fills the cavern. She exposed her desires to me and I crushed them under my boot.

Eventually she finds her way to bed, and I wait until she's fallen asleep before I lie down, dreading tomorrow.

The next morning, while the captain is still asleep, I check outside. The whipping sand hasn't abated. I curse under my breath and return to my bedroll, thinking I might just go back to napping. Not like there's anything else to do here but use the chamber pot, bathe, and eat, and the chamber pot business has been incredibly awkward between us since the beginning.

When I return to the ashes of the fire with my lit torch, the captain is sitting there, staring down at it.

"Get the fuel, Lieutenant," she barks at me, and I jump with surprise. "Start this fire."

I glare at her. This is an abrupt change. "Why don't you do it?" I ask.

"Why don't you do it, *sir*," she corrects me. My blood starts to grow hot at her demanding tone. "Don't question me. Just start it."

Incensed, I get up and do as she asks, grumbling to myself the entire time. She sits down calmly and begins to eat while I start the fire. The pile of wood has decreased steadily, and I don't know how long the storm will last. We probably can't stand this much longer.

"Our supplies are running low," I tell her.

"Then we had better use them sparingly. We'll only light the fire long enough today for the basic necessities." Her voice is firm. "Get all of your bathing and shitting out of the way now."

"All right," I say, uncertain. I knew that I was closing a door in her face, but now she has shut me out in return and locked it.

"All right, *sir*," she corrects me again.

I grit my teeth. "All right, sir."

This is what I told her I wanted, so why does it make me ache so badly?

No. This is how things are supposed to be. This is the correct order. This is right.

She says nothing to me that isn't absolutely necessary, and her voice is cold as a stone when she does speak. Instead of abating my lust, all it does is add tinder to the fire. The contrast of her body's soft edges with her sharp tongue makes my groin ache for her. Even more do I want to push her down and take off her clothes and then, she can tell me what she wants me to do, and I would do it. If she asked me to suck on her, I would lap at her nipples like I was starving. If she asked me to pleasure her, I would stick my tongue inside her and fuck her with it until she was writhing. If she wanted more, if she wanted all of me, I would give it to her.

Instead, I obey her orders as they come, and my cock stays warm and thick and just barely restrained. By the end of what must be our third day here and she's ordered me once more to check that the storm hasn't abated, I'm so tense and horny that I can barely sit down.

The fire dies. "Leave it," she tells me the moment I get up to retrieve more wood. "That's all we can risk for today."

"Yes, sir."

I return to the bedroll and lie on my back for what feels like an eternity, staring up into the darkness. Her breathing slows, and eventually turns even and quiet. Once I'm certain that she's asleep, I untie my breeches and reach inside, pulling myself out. All I have to do is conjure the image of her drying her naked body and I'm thick and solid again.

Starting with my hand at the very base of my cock, I pull it slowly up to the top, allowing the skin to encompass the head. Then I slide it back down again, spreading my dripping seed around to lubricate each stroke. I imagine what Captain Mastair looks like between the legs, and speed up my hand. My breath hitches as I picture her small cunt, dripping for me, awaiting me. As more liquid gathers at the slit at the end of my cock, my strokes make a wet sound.

"What are you doing, Lieutenant?" a harsh voice asks in the dark.

My hand freezes.

"Nothing," I respond in the same tone. "Sir."

"Don't lie to me." Even though I can't see her, I can picture her scowling face. "You speak of inappropriateness, but then you do this?" Her voice breaks just the smallest amount at the end, and I know then that she's insulted. She more or less offered herself, and instead of accepting, now I'm jerking myself off a matter of feet away from her.

"I have needs," I growl.

"As do I, and yet I've controlled them." Her irritation just fuels me. I start to move my hand again, not sure what I intend to do, but wanting to see how far I can push her.

"Lieutenant!" I hear her get up in her bedroll. I love her voice as it grows angrier, and even more of my come seeps out in anticipation. "Must I ask you directly?"

"To what?" I ask, pumping myself faster.

"To stop this." She sounds less sturdy and more breathless. "It's an order."

Now my balls are tightening up underneath me. "You order me to stop?" I ask, and my strokes become quite audible.

"I do! At once!" Though her volume is rising, the quivering of her voice gives away that she's aroused.

"You don't want me touching myself?" I can't stifle my groan. "What are you going to do about it, all the way out here? You can't stop me."

She snarls, and the click of her boots on the cave floor comes towards me. I sit up a little, my hand never leaving my cock, and continue to stroke. I didn't think it was possible for it to swell up any more, but it does.

Then, out of nowhere, she hits me across the face. It's hard and firm and surprisingly powerful. My head twists to one side, her strike taking me completely by surprise.

"Fuck," I hiss, dropping my cock.

"Disobedient shit. I'm going to throw you in a cell the moment we're back in Attirex."

Her hand across my face has lit my entire body on fire. The sting makes my cock throb harder.

"Fine," I say. "Do what you please. Just stop interrupting me." She can hit me all she wants—it will only strengthen my resolve, and make me even harder for her. I bring my hand back to my shaft and let out a groan as I pump it again. The captain's breath is coming faster, and even in the dark I can picture her face, her eyes enraged but heavy with desire, her round lips parted.

Then, a hand lands on mine, and I still. Zirelle's tiny fingers peel my own away from my cock, and I let them fall until only her small, soft palm is wrapped around me.

"You're doing it all wrong." She drags her hand up my length. Unbidden, a groan escapes me. She's squeezing me tight as she brings her fingers up to the base of the head, then back down again to the root.

My voice comes out clogged and throaty. "Then show me how it's done, Captain."

CHAPTER 7

ZIRELLE

This infernal orc.

What am I doing right now with my hand around his cock? Even though I can't see anything in this darkness, I don't need to. I can feel how huge it is and I'm going to embrace that fully. Without the light of the moon or the flickering flame of a torch to witness it, this almost doesn't feel real—like I could pretend tomorrow that it never happened.

I bring my other hand up to join my first, letting one stroke him up and then down again, while the other wraps tightly around the base.

"This is what you're supposed to do," I tell him, my voice unyielding.

Agkar groans again. "Is it? I'm not sure."

I tighten my grip and he lets out another noise of pleasure. I keep pumping, harder, pushing his skin up over his head and then back down again. I'm being rough with him, I know—but he likes it, his hips jolting up into my hands with every other stroke. I run my fingers over the slick head and then back down, bringing his moisture with me and spreading it everywhere.

That's when I feel his huge hand on my thigh. He runs it up to my hip, around to my ass. As he buries his fingers into my soft flesh, my hold on his cock gets firmer and he lets out another moan. I'm squeezing him within an inch of his life and he's eating it up.

But this isn't enough. No, now I want him touch me more, to keep reaching until his fingers are between my legs.

There's one more thing I need to do to show him how wrong he is, and how I'm much better I am at getting him off than his hand. I lean down, pulling his cock's head toward my mouth.

The second my tongue touches the lieutenant's exposed flesh, he gasps, and his whole body arches towards me. "Captain," he grunts. "Is this supposed to be a punishment?"

"Keep your mouth shut." I slide my lips onto him, taking the whole crown in my mouth. He's much bigger than anyone else I've had, and I almost can't take the entirety of his girth between my lips. I keep both hands on the shaft, moving them in time with my sucking. Agkar groans again and rocks his hips underneath me.

I stop and circle him with my tongue, continuing to pump with my fingers. I slide one palm down so I'm cupping his balls, and they're much bigger than I expected. Huge, even. I gently massage each one and Agkar's grunts speed up.

I'm going to suck this damned orc until he never, ever dreams of defying me again.

Again I sink my mouth down, and again he responds with a buck of his hips. His hand is traveling across every part of my hip and butt, testing it all out, feverishly squeezing and showing me exactly how he wants to be touching me elsewhere. He is breaking under my power.

His growls rise higher in his throat as I swallow more and more of him, and I can feel his sac tightening in my palm. So I slow down and carefully pull my mouth away, leaving just my tongue teasing the tip of him.

Agkar snarls in frustration when I stop, and his hand digs into my ass like a claw. I wait until his orgasm slips away and then I begin again.

"Yes," I say after the second time he gets close to coming, and I release him from my mouth. He lets out a strangled sound. "This *is* your punishment." I want him to be elsewhere when he reaches his limit.

Then, suddenly, there are hands on my shoulders and Agkar is pushing me backward, onto the nearest bedroll. I let out a cry of surprise and resist his firm shove, but right away he lets me go. No, he's much more interested in my pants.

"Lieutenant!" I admonish as he unlaces me. I could reach down and push him away—but why would I? This is all I've wanted. All I've desired. Everything I imagined when I brought my hand down between my legs.

"Captain," he grunts back, pulling down my pants roughly. I bring my knees up and help kick them off. "You've not seen punishment yet."

Soon each of his huge, powerful hands is wrapped around one of my thighs, and he pulls them apart. He's not rough, like I expected; he spreads me gently, and then I feel his hot breath right on the soft center between my legs. Every hair on my body stands up as he remains there, only an inch or two away from my warm sex, and I hear him breathe in deeply. There's a rumble of pleasure in his chest, and then, his mouth is on me.

I can't help gasping as he traces my edges with his tongue, exploring me in my entirety until he reaches my clit and there, he pauses. Much more softly he licks it, and when my body twitches in response, he does it again. And again. Before I realize it, I'm moaning under each insistent stroke of his tongue.

"Is that right?" he says in a low, rumble that's tinged with amusement. "You like that, Captain?"

I grab his hair and shove his head down. "Put that mouth to good use." He chuckles into me, and drops back to my entrance. There, he circles it, ducking in with just the tip of his tongue for a brief moment, then returning to my clit.

Almost right away I feel the swell of my climax creeping in, and I don't want to give him the satisfaction, not this easily. But Agkar is teasing it out anyway as he returns his attention to my sensitive nub, and something calloused and round nudges at my wet opening, slicking around the edge. His finger pushes past how tight I am, not rough, but firm. It's big, bigger than I expected, and it takes me a moment to adjust as he continues to lick, ghostly brushes against my clit. It's sinful how good he feels.

Then the finger starts to move. His tongue is rubbing harder, faster, and I'm moaning underneath him. My impending climax is filling the darkness with a swirling, sparkling light. His mouth and hand work in perfect tandem, leading me by a bridle to the cliff's edge.

"Lieutenant!" I'm whimpering and I can't help it. I want to finish so badly. His finger begins stroking, up and down inside me while his mouth imitates the motion outside, and I'm done for. My channel tightens up like iron around his hand, but Agkar doesn't let it stop him, not for a second. He just continues to lap me up while I crest, and it's like a shot of a blunderbuss going off in my head.

But the torrent I was expecting—no, it's still buried inside me. He doesn't stop his hand or mouth moving, even as I twitch and rock my hips, unconsciously trying to hide my sensitive parts from him.

"No," he growls, using his other hand to reach underneath my hips and pull me back. "You're not done."

His single finger is joined by another one, and it stretches me so far wide that I wriggle under him. I'm still tight from my orgasm, and I gasp when they both fit inside.

His mouth is back again, and I have to hold on tight to his hair not to be swept away. Every last inch of me is powerfully overstimulated and he knows it. He exploits it, sucking hard and then releasing, over and over, while his large fingers move together. I'm certain that when I do hit the ceiling, I'll pop like a waterskin and spill everywhere.

I understand my punishment now.

Agkar

She tastes like the most magical flower, like water when you're dying of thirst. Her musk fills my nose, seeping into every part of my body and filling it up with need. My hands want to squeeze her; my cock wants to fuck her; my arms want to hold her tight and still underneath me while I make her scream.

It's not difficult to bring her to her tipping point again—all I have to do is devour her, slicking my fingers in and out of her slippery cunt over and over, until she's whimpering and swallowing my hand and convulsing around me. I don't wait for her to finish before I continue, maintaining the same steady pace as before. She writhes, and I have to hold her tight to keep her underneath me.

"Oh, I can't!" She's begging, but I know she has more to give.

"Stop whining." I haven't made her explode yet. So I keep going, licking her sensitive nub, exploring her folds, all while my hand fucks her. The captain is moaning with every breath now, and she's so, so tight. I move my fingers faster, alternating strokes, as her voice rises higher and higher.

That's when I'm rewarded. She shrieks and her hole clenches around me, releasing a stream of warm liquid across my hand. There we go. My prize.

After swallowing it all down with a hunger, I lazily drag my tongue across her again, making her shake and tremble.

It's time.

While I give the captain a few moments to recover, I find my way to one of the torches in the darkness, and locate the fire-starter. She gasps when it lights up the room.

"I told you," she warns. "We have to save—"

"I want to look at you," I interrupt. "No—I am going to look at you while I'm inside you."

Her breath stops and her eyes go wide. I know she wants it because she doesn't move a muscle, simply staring as I hang up the torch on the wall and advance towards her. I pull my jerkin off over my head, and her eyes jump from my throat to my groin, taking me in.

Good. I know she likes what she sees. She's been imagining it, just like I've been imagining this.

The captain's own hands go to down to the front buttons of her shirt, and she has to redirect her focus to get them off. But the moment her big breasts are exposed to the air, dark nipples already hardening in the cool cavern, I'm on top of her. She gasps as I take one of those nipples in my mouth.

"Lieutenant," she groans. Her hand finds its way around my neck, and as my tongue twirls around her nipple, she pulls me closer. I nip with my teeth, and then soothe again with my tongue, and I know by the jerk of her hips what she really wants.

Once I've paid attention to both of her swollen nipples, I lean back and admire her. She's breathing hard, the rounded globes of her breasts moving in time with her lungs. Her cunt is still wet, and it's darker than the rest of her, hidden under black, curly hair.

I know where I belong now.

Kneeling between her legs, my length still hard and swollen and ready for her, I reach down and stroke myself. Her eyes are liquid with desire.

"Do you want it, Captain?" I ask her, running my hand up and down my cock again. A strand of seed spills onto her belly and her breath shivers. "Tell me. Tell me how much you want me to fuck you."

She swallows hard, and her fists clench tight like she's desperate to touch me but won't allow herself the privilege. Her desire only makes the scent of her richer and sweeter.

"Lieutenant," she says, reaching down between her legs to spread her folds for me. I've never seen anything as delicious in my life as her exposed slit, dripping and shining for me. "You had better do it right now."

I pull her legs apart, and rub the head of my cock through her juices. Now I'm slick and ready for her. "Yes, sir."

CHAPTER 8

ZIRELLE

Agkar the orc is beautiful, I'll admit that. His chest is broad and thick with muscle, all coiled up and tense while he manhandles his impressive cock. There are three huge scars across his chest that I imagine were once ugly, bloody gashes. His hips are powerful and his groin has two sharp lines that wind down from his hips to his balls, showing off just how hard and fast he'll be able to fuck me. He drags my slickness all around with his cockhead, and each stroke sends off a shower of sparks behind my eyes.

He looks down there just like I'd hoped—no, he's even more generous. All I can think about is how he'll feel inside me.

"Hold on, Captain," he whispers, and that's when he finally gives me what I've been craving. His head prods me, and when he finds my pussy pliable from his repeated ministrations, he pushes inside.

I have no choice but to hold on. Agkar is big, far bigger than his two fingers together, and my body has to stretch to fit him.

I grab his forearms and clench, gasping as he meets resistance. All of his tongue-fucking has left me tight. But Agkar doesn't force his way in. Instead he starts to thrust, just the tip of him in and out, and damn, does it feel good. Amazing. Each small taste of him shoots a lightning bolt up through me right into my throat, and soon, my sheath relaxes, welcoming him in.

The moment I'm ready, Agkar is inside me. He sinks in as far as he can in one stroke, and I can't bite back a cry as I swallow up as much of him as possible. I've never felt so completely, thoroughly, and obscenely full. He rests there for a moment to get his breath back, barely holding himself up above me, veins engorged all along his arms. His form is so broad and vast that I'm dwarfed by it. I'm gasping underneath him, relishing the feel of him buried inside me while still so impossibly thick.

"Fuck," Agkar hisses to himself. I spent so much time bringing him to the edge and back that he's still there, almost ready to erupt. I'm proud of myself. I wrap my legs around his hips and gently pull him in deeper, if that were possible. His groan is immense and guttural, and I wonder if he'll go off like a firework that got lit by accident. I want to feel him surge inside me, to watch his face as I wring him out.

"Captain..." His voice is tight and quiet. "If you do that, it won't last."

"Then you'll just have to do it again a second time," I hiss back. A new fire lights in the lieutenant's eyes, and he withdraws almost all the way, only to slam inside me again. It feels like the world is tilting, and I'm cascading around with it as my huge orc strokes all the way in and out at a slow, severe pace. When I look down, I see that not all of him can fit inside me—there's more of his cock still, spreading my folds wide. His tip drags along the inside of me with each stroke, lighting up every crease and fold of me with bliss.

When he leans forward to change his angle, he slips even further in and I cry out. How I have anything left to give is a mystery to me, but I'm so sopping wet around him that there's no resistance as he continues driving me higher and higher up into the sky. With both hands I reach around and firmly grab his ass, the muscle hard as stone under my fingers. Agkar gasps on top of me and instinctually quickens his pace, and I feel like I might just spring apart underneath him. Each thrust is stoking my fire and I'm starting to boil over.

"That's right, Captain," he mutters, grinning wickedly. There's a bright coil winding its way around me that's beginning to squeeze in tight. Soon, my finish begins to swirl upward from where his cock is buried and into my belly, then my chest. Everything in the universe is focused on this single place where our bodies connect.

"Faster, Lieutenant," I moan, grabbing hold of my tits as they bounce wildly, plucking at my own nipples.

"Yes, sir." He cranks up the speed and I'm lost, squirming under every thrust, sending me floating higher and higher into the air. I'm crying out now, the bedroll cinched up under my back while this magnificent orc takes me.

Then, he lets out a guttural roar that sounds like he's close to his tipping point. "Don't you go over yet," I growl to him. Agkar snarls something unintelligible back, some Trollkin word I've never heard before. As I drift closer to the finish line my cries get sharper and louder, driven by the slick, wet sound of his cock ramming inside me. Never have I felt like this, stretched wide, completely enthralled and made of pure, blistering sensation.

That's when my orgasm rushes me hard and fast, and it flings me up and into the air. It's like I'm high above us, looking down as Agkar groans with pleasure, and his enormous cock swells up. My channel is squeezing so tight that he has a hard time yanking himself out, and with one final thrust into the air, he's gushing white, sticky fluid across my belly.

When I finally return to my body, I can see stars across the dark cavern ceiling, flashing in time with the pulse of my blood. Agkar falls to his elbows on top of me, panting, sweat dripping off one of his tusks. My belly is slick with his seed, so our bodies are both covered in it now, but he doesn't seem to care.

I'm surprised he withdrew. Humans and orcs aren't compatible like that, are we? But I feel like he knows something that I don't, and so I resist asking the question because making any sound now would break this hushed moment of intimacy between us. It feels as if perhaps a wall has come down. His mouth is only inches away from mine, and it wouldn't take much to simply tilt my head up and kiss him.

No. This was just a desperate fuck borne out of a mutual need for release. A way to pass the time, to spend our pent-up energy, to finally dissolve this festering lust between us. The desire to have something more is just a natural rush.

Finally Agkar falls down next to me, and strangely, all I want is to roll over and bury my face in his shoulder, inhaling the warm, musky scent of him. His arm would curl around me, bringing me close in to his chest—

This urge takes me by surprise. That is much too personal, far too intimate. I've taken plenty of strange men home with me and never felt the need to cuddle afterwards, but right now, that's all I crave.

I cannot act on it. I can't show this kind of desire in front of the lieutenant.

So we lie there side-by-side, breathing heavily, neither of us saying a word. Eventually, Agkar rises to his feet and pulls his breeches back on, and that's when I know that the tryst is over. There will be no embraces, no tenderness. The door closes heavily in front of me, and I can't help feeling deflated as I get up and button my shirt, then clean myself off and lace my pants, which is awkward to do with my wobbly legs. Oh, will I be sore tomorrow.

While Agkar puts his shirt back on, carefully keeping his attention anywhere besides me, I get out of the bedroll he was using before and return to my own, feeling oddly off-kilter. He puts out the torch, and everything goes dark.

There's an emptiness inside of me that wasn't there before, and I'm not sure that this is what I wanted.

AGKAR

I just fucked the captain so hard that she screamed my name. I'm not even certain if she realized what she was doing, and it drove me into a pure frenzy. Her small, supple body under mine was a blessing. How she fiercely clutched my ass, driving into me just as much as I was ramming myself into her—it was intoxicating. I might have been on top of her, but she had control. The way she squeezed me tight almost made it impossible to pull out of her at the last minute, but the last thing I need is to impregnate my superior officer. That would be a right mess and a half.

I don't like the look on her face as I put my clothes back on. Maybe I should have done something else to show her how marvelous she'd been. But this was just a small, temporary dalliance, wasn't it? Something we both clearly needed. So why do I feel like I should have laid down next to her, pulled her into my arms and kissed her sweaty forehead? I could almost smell that was what she wanted, too. She may be hard as stone on the outside, but I can see that inside, my captain is as soft as velvet.

It's not what I expected to find there.

Now we've silently returned to our beds and it's much too late. I stare at the ceiling for an eternity, long after Zirelle's breaths have evened out. I reckon this feeling has nothing to do with the captain. It's the part of me that still hungers after Nera, that wishes I'd made her mine. I could have slept next to her every night if I had just...

I stop the thought in its tracks, because I know it would never have gone that way. She did not choose me, and that wouldn't have changed if I'd freed her myself. Even if I had won the Narzag-kig, she would never have been my mate. She was already bound to another.

There's a swirling, empty hole inside my chest that perhaps I could have filled if I had simply pressed my face into Zirelle's soft, curly hair. Instead, I pretended like this was nothing— just a business transaction.

I do manage to fall asleep eventually, but my dreams are all full of Captain Mastair, keening underneath me as I fuck her over and over again.

I'm awoken the next morning by the captain stomping down the tunnel. She emerges into the main cavern, her expression cool and sharp.

"The storm has abated," she says in a clipped tone. She has returned to her old self.

It's finally over. We'll be free from this forced cohabitation at last. I sit up quickly and locate the long dagger she gave me along with the sword I brought on our original journey. Who knows when the Black Fox will return now? It's only a matter of time.

"Will we wait for them, sir?" I ask. I don't want to earn her ire today. This is how I will express my gratitude for the gift she gave me last night.

"Yes. We'll keep the fire out and the torch unlit, and wait for their return." She gestures to the cave entrance. "I'll be on this side, and you'll be over there. As soon as we hear them, be prepared to launch a surprise attack."

She gives me detailed instructions about how we'll manage to take all five of them together. It's a smart plan, picking them off silently one at a time as they enter the cavern, hoping that they'll be none the wiser until it's too late.

"Dead or alive, it doesn't matter to me," she says. "As long as the Black Fox is no longer a concern of mine."

I nod and then we put out the torch, taking up our positions to either side of the cavern entrance. Who knows how long we'll have to wait here in the dark until our targets make their return?

"Captain, I—" I begin.

"Silence," she hisses. "We cannot give ourselves away prematurely."

I'm not even sure what I wanted to say. That I was sorry for not taking her into my arms when I should have? We both knew it was just a casual fuck when we began.

So we wait in the darkness, in total silence, while I try not to imagine her naked legs curled around my waist in ecstasy while she moans my name.

CHAPTER 9

ZIRELLE

I shouldn't blame the lieutenant for an expectation that wasn't there, and yet I can't stop thinking about how he smelled like strength and sex, or how perfectly full he made me, as if our bodies were designed for each other. I wanted to take those handsome lips in mine, to feel his arms wrapping around me, to fall asleep curled into his huge, broad chest. There's a sprout of resentment that feels used and discarded after the moment we shared, and it wants to punish him for something he didn't do wrong.

We stand there in the dark, not speaking, for what feels like hours before we hear the sound of voices. They echo in the small tunnel. There are clearly a few of them, and I hope that our assumption about their numbers based on the bedrolls is correct. We'll try to keep things quiet as we pick them off so they don't turn and run. The last thing we need is for one to escape intact and keep the operation going elsewhere.

Light bobs closer as they approach. I can see the outline of

Agkar's carved features, his proud nose and sharp brows and the tusks that curl up over his top lip all highlighted in orange.

"I thought we might never see this place again," one of them is saying. "Maybe we should find another camp that isn't so far out."

"I don't think we could find one as good as this," another answers. "They'll never find us here."

The first one steps into the cavern, and he's looking straight ahead, not noticing either of us standing a few feet off to each side. They aren't suspicious—not at all. I hold up a finger to my lips, giving Agkar a firm look so he doesn't attack too soon. We can't let them escape by giving them a heads-up.

The second one follows close behind, and then a third and a fourth. There's one woman and three men, all human, and at least one more in the tunnel. But they're taking their time, and we can't wait any longer or they'll spot us before we can attack. I hold one dagger in each hand and lunge, burying the first blade into a man's back. Before the others can turn around, I've got my second dagger in the woman, right through her throat so she can't scream. I'm grateful now for all those years of combat training when I was still a private.

Behind me, I hear the second man shout as Agkar grabs him and drives his sword through the man's gut. I'll have to talk to him about that later, because that's not how you kill someone in silence.

Shit. I hope the noise hasn't scared off the fifth one.

Sure enough, inside the tunnel, there's a telltale flash of a torch as the last man turns and runs. I sprint after him as fast as I can, but he has longer legs than I do. No, I can't let him escape. Not after sitting here in the dark for three days. The lieutenant would never let me live it down.

So I bring back my dagger over my head and fling it as hard as I can.

There's a cry as it sticks in his shoulder blades. He doesn't stop running, but he slows down, and I'm able to leap onto him with my other dagger ready. It sinks into the back of his neck, the sharp blade sliding right through him, and he lets out a terrible gurgle as blood gushes out of the wound.

Someone is running towards me. I rip the dagger out of his throat and turn to attack whoever else might be fleeing the scene—but it's Agkar, panting, and for a moment he looks concerned. I lower my weapon as he surveys my victim.

Then, a smile flicks onto his wide mouth. "We got them all," he says, wonder in his voice. "And one back there is still alive."

That's better than I could have hoped for. He picks up the body of the man I just killed and drags it back into the cavern, and we pile up all four of them together. The man I had to chase down was the face of the Black Fox, the man on the posters. Another man lies on his side on the floor, groaning and moaning as he bleeds. Agkar only injured him in the side —enough to disable him, but not enough to kill him. As we stand over our work together, I turn to my compatriot and nod in acknowledgment, feeling immensely pleased with our work.

The Black Fox is done at last.

"We did it. Good job, Lieutenant."

"Thank you, Captain." There's not even a trace of impertinence in his voice.

I proceed to coming up with our next plan. We'll tie up our one surviving prisoner and drag him back to Attirex with us, leaving the other bodies and the loot here. Then we'll ride back with greater numbers and a few camels to empty out the cavern, returning what goods we can to their respective owners.

Our man is mostly unconscious, so the lieutenant fixes him

up enough to survive the trip home with his curious med kit, and slings the body over his shoulder.

"He's not too heavy?" I ask. I wouldn't be able to carry half of this grown man.

"No. Not for me." Agkar's muscles flex as he shifts our captive into a comfortable position, and then he heads for the exit. As we depart, I glance back at the cave. In a strange way, I will miss it.

AGKAR

Oh, am I glad to see the sunlight, even if it's harsh and searing hot. As we leave the cavern in the desert behind us, a small part of me is also loathe to return to the real world.

Something was different there. The captain changed in front of my me from my irritating superior officer to a soft, pliable, sensual woman. I wonder if I had kissed her, would she have been just as open and willing?

I'll never know now. I had the opportunity, and I didn't take it. But that's for the best. It was transactional, something we did merely to resolve the tension between us, and now we won't need to ever speak of it again.

Yet I steal the occasional glance at her as we walk, making sure to look away quickly so she doesn't notice. We head back to Attirex in silence, side by side. Maybe I should fall back again so I can look at her ass as she climbs over one dune and then the next, but that would surely be too obvious.

If anything, this tryst in the desert has taught me something about myself. I want someone who I can fall asleep next to, someone I can fuck every night and fatten up with my whelps. Someone small and soft like Zirelle, who gives easily to my hands, and clings on tight with her legs while I pump her full of my seed.

Someone who isn't forbidden to me.

At least we secured her victory here today. She can dangle this man for everyone to see, calling him an accomplice of the Black Fox, and return the valuables that were stolen. Her reputation in the city will be restored. Perhaps this achievement will convince her that she is enough, and she will stop staying late into the night and drinking herself into oblivion. That was a small thing I could do in return for the experience of burying myself inside her.

"We're here," the captain says as we crest a dune. Sprawled out below us are the brightly-colored tents of Attirex. This city is like Zirelle herself: An unexpected jewel in the middle of a desert.

The guards meet us at the gate, and there's much cheering and celebrating once the captain explains where we've been. This was a big victory for the city guard.

But she doesn't believe in celebrating. In fact, she barely allows us a breather, and early the next morning we gear up to return to the cave, outfitted with camels and carts, to bring back what the Black Fox took.

Life will return to normal after this. There will be no more adventures across the desert, trapped in a small space with the captain through long, dark nights.

ZIRELLE

I did it. At last, I can scratch one more item off of my to-do list.

Our merchants are glad to have their things returned, even if it's not all there. The Black Fox must have been selling off what they could to other criminal enterprises, or perhaps through a storefront of their own in the city. There are always other troublemakers hiding under the surface in Attirex, and I'll weed each of them out the same way.

Except that I wasn't the one who thought to look out in the desert. It was Lieutenant Agkar who handed me my redemption on a silver platter. Perhaps I should thank him.

No. He was simply doing his job as my serving officer.

Soon work returns to as normal a state as there ever has been. There's something new to attend to every day, ongoing paperwork that never seems to run out, and a crisis here and there to keep things interesting. I haven't fallen back on the drink again, not yet—but after Agkar confronted me about it, I want to keep it that way.

Between the lieutenant and me, however, the atmosphere is cool and tense in a much different way than before. Agkar's changed since we returned from our adventure in the desert. He obeys my commands without question, and there is no more impertinent shine in his eyes as he answers them all with a *sir*. Now he remembers to request permission to enter my office. He has been learning Freysian words here and there, and trying his best to use them.

Rarely does he meet my gaze.

I miss the way he used to give me an obstinate look with those strange, green-gold eyes when I made a request. At least then I felt like *someone* to him. He bucked my authority because he saw me as a human woman, like her. Now he only sees me as his captain, his superior officer, and there's nothing else between us. I understood that when we returned to our beds without a word in the Black Fox's cave.

It certainly makes my job easier, but I don't sleep any better. It's been a struggle not to delve into my wine stores, but I can't give him, or any of the other trollkin, more reasons to doubt my leadership. I visit a healer for a remedy that will make it easier not to fall back into the drink, and yet still I hunger for it, for the peace and relief it brings.

I should be glad. This is what I wanted—his obedience. Instead, my chest tightens whenever he nods and marches away to execute my orders.

Which one of us was truly punished that night?

I think about it more evenings than not when I'm trying to fall asleep. As the commanding officer I live outside the barracks, so I can make all the noise I like without anyone around to hear me. But nothing fills me up as much as the lieutenant did. No, as *Agkar* did. The hole my orc has left inside me is looming and vast.

My orc. The thought is ridiculous, and yet I loathe the idea of him being with anyone else.

I could go to him. I could ask him to fuck me again and take me to that deep, dark place we found together in the cavern. Would he do it? Or would he scoff at the idea?

There's no way I'd risk being humiliated like that. He already refused me once, and it burned deep. Asking for a repeat would be admitting defeat, confessing that I've developed a need for him beyond that one night. Not to mention I can't be caught by one of the other soldiers sneaking in and out of the lieutenant's room.

Perhaps I can find my release elsewhere, away from all these ugly feelings I keep having about him.

One night I go out to the tavern late and sit at the bar top in my civilian clothes, pretending to drink my wine while I look over my prospects. There aren't that many people here besides a few human men and two trollkin. None of the men have even the slightest sex appeal. There's a troll sitting in one corner, sipping on his beer at the open window. He has gold earrings, gold necklaces, even a few rings on his fingers. I'd bet that he has a dick as big as Agkar's, if not bigger.

Would I even dare make a move? Trolls and orcs look different, of course, being two separate varieties of trollkin. But it's the feel of a huge body on top of mine that I'm after, isn't it? I want that enormous cock shoving me wide open and then filling me up to the brim, like Agkar did, and I think a troll would do just fine.

Eventually I stand up and make my way to the next table at the window. The troll glances up curiously from his drink, looking me over like he's waiting for me to make trouble. Humans and trollkin don't even sit near each other when we have a choice about it—I know that my voluntary move is raising an alarm bell in his mind.

I close my eyes and lean back, letting the cool air blow in and tousle my hair. I'm just here to enjoy the breeze the same as he is. After a while I sense the troll relax, and he continues drinking in silence.

There must be some way to break the ice that won't send him running. I turn slightly in his direction, letting my eyes linger on his face long enough that he realizes I'm staring. I wonder if it's just Agkar who's attracted to humans, or are other trollkin, too? I suppose I'm about to find out.

The troll doesn't look away, but there's confusion in his face. I study him. His features are different, but not too dissimilar from Agkar's as to make him seem completely foreign. His skin is a purplish-blue, and his tusks are quite a bit longer than an orc's. I could see myself getting on top of him if that's what it takes to fill this void inside me.

I learn forward just a little, and raise my hand to the side of my mouth like I want to speak quietly to him. Eyebrows furrowed, he slides forward in his seat until he's close enough that he'll be able to hear me if I whisper.

"Are you waiting for anyone?" I ask. He looks surprised that I'm speaking fluent Trollkin.

Then he shakes his head. "No. Why?" There's a spark of suspicion in his eye.

"Because I'm looking for someone to go home with."

At first it seems like he doesn't understand what I'm saying. Then realization dawns, and suspicion morphs into mischief. This time when he surveys me, he looks like a predator sizing up prey.

Oh, yes. He wants me.

"I've never been propositioned by a human before," he says, voice low so no one can overhear us.

"Now you have." I wait expectantly for his answer.

"If that's what she wants," he says, sucking down the last of his beer, "then that's what she'll have."

Chapter 10

Agkar

She really did put me in my place, I think, as I nod my head at one of her orders and rush to comply with it. The other trollkin soldiers give me strange looks as I walk away to do the captain's bidding without even a question.

She is the one in charge here, and I must remember that. If I don't, I will walk out to her house, let myself in her front door, and push her down to her bed so I can make her scream again. As the days wear on, that's all I want: To lick her between her legs until she's writhing and begging me to stop, and then while she's still tight and tender, slide my cock inside her one inch at a time until I'm buried in her perfect sheath. Then, I'd press her lush, full lips to mine.

If I remember for a moment that she is my superior, I can bury this urge for a day longer. I will simply continue this way, one day at a time, until I can forget.

Unfortunately, every time I see her that seems to be more

and more impossible. I can only think of her mouth open in a perfect circle as I fucked her, the bounce of her breasts underneath me as I brought her to her stunning finish. I think of her walking into that pool of water, of her hand wrapped around mine, ordering me to stop. I think of her running after the Black Fox and throwing a dagger through his back, fierce and determined and beautiful.

Every time she tells me what to do, my gut tightens and it takes everything in my power not to get hard. I distract myself by obeying her every command and working my hardest to do the job well. I've even started asking the human officers to explain new Freysian words to me. At night, I jerk off until I'm spilling all over my cot, and then do it again and again, imagining my hand is her perfect cunt instead.

One morning, the captain walks through the big room where we search baggage. She has a spring in her step I haven't seen before, not since we returned from the Black Fox bust. Her dark eyes look alive.

I know then that she's fucked someone else. It's clear from the new shine on her cheeks, the way her scent reeks of sex. She's taken to bed someone who isn't *me*.

A black pit forms in my abdomen, and maddening jealousy rises up to the surface like a sea creature. The intensity of it takes me by surprise.

She stops when she sees me, her eyes losing that little bit of light. Her posture becomes stiff and formal. "Lieutenant," she says, tilting her chin to acknowledge me. "There's a big load of cargo coming in that was flagged as suspicious."

I nod. "I'll handle it, sir." But what I really want to say is, *who was it?* I want to track down whoever put his cock inside my female and bury my sword in his chest.

The urge is so strong it nearly overpowers me.

"Thank you." The captain glances around the room one last

time while I try to squash my violent fury. How could she look elsewhere for what she needs when I am standing right here, doing her bidding day in and day out without question?

No. She is *mine*. My muscles are quivering with irrational, unspent rage as she turns and stalks out of the room, her mood significantly dampened. I can't bear the idea of anyone on top of my captain but me.

Why? Why did she go somewhere else? I would have satisfied her and beyond.

Never again. I will just have to show her that I'm the best choice—that it should be me inside her every night.

I decide it without a conscious thought. My woman, my human, will only smell of me from now on.

That night, after the daytime shift is over, I watch the captain return to her house. I follow along not too far behind, but far enough that she won't catch sight of me unless she looks back, and I keep my footfalls quiet.

I'm not sure what I'm hoping to discover. Maybe her new lover will be there and I can find out who's taken my place. Then I'll track him down, rip his head from his shoulders, and plant it upon a pike as a warning to everyone else.

When she walks inside and closes the door behind her, there are no telltale sounds of greeting. Maybe I was wrong, and there is no one else. Maybe this is all something I made up after seeing one look on her face and resenting how she could seem so happy and alive without it being me who made her feel that way.

Now that I'm here, looking in her window, I want to be in there with her. She stands up and starts to remove her captain's coat, then lets it fall from her shoulders. I want to unbutton her undershirt and reveal the treasure underneath. She reaches for her trousers, and then seems to sense someone is watching because she comes to the window and closes it, drawing the curtains.

Damn.

I can't continue on pretending that I don't want her—all of her. I should never have left the bedroll that night. My need is an ocean, and the only thing that will save my soul is having Zirelle again, ranks be damned.

But I'm not going to handle her like I did last time. I will fix my mistake. I'm going to worship every inch of her, peel her one layer at a time until she wants nothing else but my hands and my mouth on her, my cock inside her.

So I walk to her door, then raise one fist to knock.

ZIRELLE

Of course I've never taken a troll to my bed before, but after Agkar, I wasn't entirely surprised by the experience. He was big, just like I had hoped, and more than willing. But every time I closed my eyes, I saw my orc instead, moving on top of me, gripping my thighs as the troll stroked in and out. I climaxed, just barely, and made him pull out right at the end. He didn't understand why, but after what Agkar had done, I just had a bad feeling.

I sent him packing afterward, which he didn't terribly mind. On his way out, Lo'zar scribbled down an address.

"I'm staying here for at least a week," he said, eyes half-lidded. "Lots of business to do, you know."

When he was gone, I crumpled up the paper and dropped

it in the trash. I was sated, for that night, and I didn't want a repeat.

No, after he left, there was only one thing I wanted: Agkar's lovely, sculpted chest over mine. His mouth between my legs, bringing me to that brilliant spot of light over and over again. There's simply no comparison. Even worse, I felt almost like I was betraying him, as little sense as that makes.

Why can't I banish him from my thoughts? At least the troll has held off my physical need for another few days, but I don't know how long that will last.

I'm ashamed when I see the lieutenant after that. He's the one I imagined while I had sex with a complete stranger. Maybe I should have gone to his quarters in the barracks, instead, and demanded a repeat of our night in the Black Fox's den.

No. I knew it would be playing with fire. If I need to find another troll or orc again, then I will.

After my shift, I undress and lie down in my hammock to sleep. It's a hot night, and I could use the fresh air.

There comes a light knock at my door. Surprised that anyone would be coming to visit me this late, I wonder if it's Lo'zar returning for another round. Hopefully he isn't that bold.

I put on my pants and shirt again, then pad to the door in my bare feet. When I open it, I'm not at all expecting to find Agkar standing on the other side. He is impressively tall, and he's abandoned his uniform, leaving just a jerkin underneath.

"Lieutenant?" I ask. I try to keep the sudden rush of excitement I feel at seeing my orc out of my voice. "What are you doing here at this hour?"

But he doesn't speak. He leans forward, propping one elbow on my doorframe, and his gaze roves from my face down to my chest, all the way to my feet. I feel a little shiver, but I know it's not the cold in this kind of weather. I'm nervous at the intensity in his eyes, and I wonder if somehow, he's found out. Does he know what I've done?

"What is it?" I'm harsher this time, uncomfortable with the look on his face. "Coming to my home this late is inappropriate."

That draws a reaction. His lip turns up on one side, and his eyebrow arches. But Agkar doesn't answer my question. Instead he lets himself inside, brushing past me. It's pure disobedience.

"Lieutenant," I warn.

He seizes me by the arm and drags me into the house, slamming the door. I'm so surprised that I let out a little yelp.

"It was all quite inappropriate, wasn't it, Zirelle?" His lips wrap around my name, and his voice is lower than anything I've heard before. He leans very close, until his mouth is almost touching my ear. "What we did."

So he's acknowledging it. It wasn't my imagination, what happened in that cavern while we waited in the dark.

"That was then," I say, hardening my voice. "This is now. There is no pretending, remember?" Here we are, back in civilization, where the hierarchy he loves so much remains intact.

But Agkar doesn't look like he believes me for a second. Still holding me by the arms, he brings me in even closer until he's staring down at me from his seven-plus feet of height. I don't pull away, even though I should.

"Yes, it is now," he says, his voice thick and heavy. "And this time, I'm going to do things right."

I'm not expecting it when he leans down and takes my mouth in his, so I gasp against him. His lips are insistent, though, pulling mine apart gently, suckling at them until they open for him. My will to even consider resisting turns to smoke as his tongue darts inside. Agkar's hand travels up to my face and pulls me in even tighter, crushing my mouth against his, his tusks pressing into my cheeks. The smell of him is everywhere and it's that same musky, heady scent as in the cave. His other hand slips down my back to my butt, and squeezes it so tight my hips are grinding his thighs. I can tell he's already hard underneath.

Has he been desiring me this whole time the way I've been desiring him?

He takes my mouth even more insistently, eating me up like a tender morsel. As he runs his hand from one round cheek of my ass to the other, I find myself groaning against his lips. His hold grows even more protective, more demanding.

This time, I'm going to do things right. Why is he kissing me now, when he didn't before? This is a wholly different version of the lieutenant. I wonder what's happened to strip off the shield he'd put up between us in the cavern.

I should turn him away. What we did was secret, taboo, unrepeatable. But oh, how his lips on mine make my body sing. This is everything I wanted then: To be held, to be kissed, to be a soft flower that Agkar could make bloom. I imagine a world where this is no mistake.

Maybe, I could let what I want become what I have.

When Agkar pulls away from me he's breathing hard, and his eyes are intense. "Where is your bed?"

All I have to do is nod in the direction of my bedroom, and he lifts me up by the hips as if I weigh nothing at all. My legs instinctively wrap around his waist, and he hums in satisfaction.

Instead of dropping me on the bed, he crouches down and lays me back on it with a surprising gentleness. He starts kissing at my jaw, then the bare flesh of my throat, where he runs his tusks down to my collar. His fingers find my belly, and slowly slide up underneath the fabric of my shirt as if he's taking careful notes of my shape. He slides down to kiss my exposed stomach, and I can't help rising up in to his hands. As he unbuttons my shirt, he attends to each new inch of skin he reveals. By the time Agkar has freed my breasts I'm gasping and soaking into my under-trousers. I want his hands there, in the empty chasm between my legs, but he's intent on taking it slow and savoring me.

This is not the orc who fucked me hard and fast in the cavern and then pretended like it never happened. What has changed?

I don't know, but I want it. I've longed for it ever since that night.

My breath shudders as he teases each of my nipples, rolling them until they're hard and tight. He gazes down fondly before he brings one into his mouth, brushing his canines over them while making sure not to break any skin.

But I'm getting impatient, and my hips flex whenever his tongue makes another pass.

"So eager, my Zirelle," he says, his hand finding its way to the laces of my pants.

Right now he is not the lieutenant, and I am not his captain. Here he is a powerful, dangerous, and virile orc who craves me just as I crave him. Now I want to see the creature who's been ruling my fantasies in all his glory.

"Your turn," I say, stopping his hand.

Agkar grins widely, pushing his tusks high up on his cheeks. "So you want to eat me up, too?" he asks as I grab the front of his jerkin. He unlaces it and pulls it up over his head so I can finally see all of him. My hands travel up his abdomen to his chest, and all the way to his tusks, drinking in every last inch of his dark green skin and taut, dense muscle.

When I've had my fill of him, Agkar draws my pants down slowly, sampling every part of my legs with his lips, even my feet. My toes curl as he runs his hands up and down the inside of my thighs, not quite touching my sex but getting so close to it that all I want is for him to move one inch farther. He's the opposite of before, suddenly intent on drawing this out as long as he possibly can, giving me intimacy, closeness, and affection. He's straining his pants but he hasn't made a move to let his huge cock spring free. No, he's paying tender attention to every last bit of me.

I need more. I need *him.*

As if hearing my wish, Agkar brushes a huge hand against the warm spot between my legs, just a teasing graze, and I twitch and jerk. He runs a finger gently over my folds, as if testing how wet I've gotten for him, and lets out a pleased, rumbling *mmm* sound.

"Oh, do you want me so much?" he asks, voice sultry.

I hesitate. Do I want to give him this kind of power over me? Not that I can really deny it, the way my body yearns for him, dripping under his fingers.

"Yes," I whisper. "I do, Agkar."

His green-gold eyes are satisfied with my response. He dips his fingers between my lower lips, sliding from my entrance to my clit and then back. My hips move of their own accord, begging him to give me more.

"Soon," Agkar says, and returns to kissing my throat, my ear, my shoulder, my nipple. His hand is torturous. All I want is for him to slip one finger inside me and give me a small sample of what it will feel like when he fills me up later. But he doesn't give in to the urgent snap of my hips. It seems like ages have passed when Agkar finally kisses his way down my chest, past my belly, to the curly hair at the base of my abdomen. He runs his fingers through it and lets out a heavy breath.

"You smell delicious," he murmurs, lust permeating his voice. "I can't wait to taste you again." His words are like caramel, and his mouth between my thighs... oh, I remember that. He's gentler this time, slow and more purposeful as he sucks on my clit. When his tongue enters me, I moan and throw my head back. It's just a tease, but it's so good that I can barely breathe. Before I reach the ceiling, he backs away and I whimper in disappointment.

"Don't worry," he says, kissing his way back up to my ear. "I'll fuck you until you can't come even once more."

I tremble with anticipation. That's all I've been wanting.

When Agkar finally removes his pants, his olive-green cock is huge and throbbing, thick veins winding their way up the sides to a dark, swollen head. His seed is already collected in the slit at the top, and his eyes are focused intently on me as I draw the liquid down and drag it around. He groans as I use both hands, and even then, my palms don't come close to filling the space between his head and his root.

How this fits inside me, I still don't understand. But I can't wait.

CHAPTER 11

AGKAR

The way she looks at me... I could never have imagined how it would feel to be gazed upon this way. Nera only ever carried fear on her face, like she was simply waiting for me to hurt her.

No, there's nothing but lust and admiration inside my little Zirelle. And it's all for me.

"You're so big," she says. I grunt as she tightens her grip on my shaft. She knows just how I like it.

I grin down at her. "I know." Gently, I take her hands away and encircle her fingers with my big palm to put on display just how much larger I am. I don't know how I fit inside her tiny body, but I'm thrilled to do it again. My cock is already drooling for her, waiting to slick her up and slide inside.

I lean down like I'm about to kiss her, but stop an inch away from her mouth.

"Tell me," I say in a growl. "Tell me how much you long to have me inside you." I need to know that she wants me as much as I want her. I need to hear the words, because I have a feeling that what we're about to do will be irreversible.

"Agkar," she says quietly. She reaches up to either side of my face, and her dark eyes bore into me. "Give it to me."

Keeping my gaze riveted to hers, I say, "Whatever my woman wishes." Then I kiss her, deep and hungry.

My human is so, so warm for me, her whole body trembling with need. But I want her to fully enjoy this, to get everything she desires out of me, so I pull her onto my lap and lean back. She has a surprised, questioning look in her eyes as my cock sits between her legs, the head pressed insistently against her belly.

"Take what you would like," I tell her, and I put my hand on my shaft, gently stroking up and down. Zirelle understands then what I'm suggesting. I get a perfect look at her body as she straddles my hips with her knees. Her powerful thighs flex as she lifts herself and reaches down to take me in her hand. Every tendon in my body is tensed and ready for her. She rubs the head around her small bud, coating both of us, and then guides it slowly to her beautiful, dark cunt. I want to see her swallow me, eat me up, rise and fall on top of me until her breasts are bouncing, but I have to go at her speed. I take her hips in my hands simply to steady her while she guides me inside her small, delicate body.

It's slow, almost painfully slow. Everything about how she feels is sublime. I could simply pull her down and jam myself in deep, give us both the desperate satisfaction we need, but I want to watch and savor her. She pauses when she's absorbed my whole tip, and her eyes close as she adjusts to my size. She's so wonderfully tight that I can't help digging my fingers into her pliant flesh. Soon she begins to move, taking only my head and nothing else. She's making high-pitched sounds already, and then her fingers drop down between her legs.

So she's going to use me for her pleasure. I can't help smirking. I maintain our modest pace while she runs her fingers across herself. She's tightening already, and her mewls grow louder. She'll be so hot and sticky with her own juices when I finally get inside her that I don't know how long I'll hold out.

Then her first peak comes, and her powerful cunt clenches around me. "Yes," I whisper, supporting her thighs as her release weakens her. "Take everything you want."

A devilish look comes over her face, and she slows us down. I let Zirelle take the lead as she guides me in further. I don't know how I can possibly fit, but I do, and her rippling squeezes are almost my undoing.

Then she raises her hips again, and once more, she touches herself. Drool pools in my mouth as I watch my cock slipping in and out of her, her folds spread impossibly wide to accommodate me. Her tiny bud is beautiful under her hands, and she's already clenching up again. It's the most exquisite bliss I could imagine.

I hold her up once more as her climax overwhelms her. This time, I take initiative and gently press in deeper.

"Oh!" Her voice is like a song. "Oh, yes!"

I will show her just how worthy I am of her body, of her heart. I will make her forget about anyone who is not me.

ZIRELLE

I have no words for how he feels, my orc. I ache for him to fill me all the way up, but I want to savor this. He's clearly holding back what he's needing for my pleasure. This version of Agkar will give me anything I want and I'll happily take it.

But my thighs are starting to wear out, so I'm relieved when he opens his eyes and draws his own fingers down to the space between us where my wet clit is waiting for him. Soon I'm standing at the edge of a precipice, and when Agkar tips me over the edge, I can't help but cry out. I glide downward, and though my channel is seizing up tight, he finally delves all the way inside.

"Say my name, sweet Zirelle," he says, voice low as a drum.

My lips can barely move as my orgasm ripples through me. "Agkar, yes!" He grunts and lifts me up with his huge hands, then brings me down hard again over his cock. I moan as it draws out my descent even further, and my legs go boneless.

"That is enough of that, little human," he says. Suddenly I'm on my back and he's yanking my thighs up to hook over his hips. Here I feel even more of his shape, gently curved upward, his head rubbing against the core of my being. His size feels like it's increased tenfold in this position. He grips me tight as he thrusts harder, shifting his angle each time. When he hits that place again I moan, and my eyes roll back into my head.

"Is that it?" he asks, voice guttural.

I can barely manage out a nod. He repeats the motion, rocking back and forth and striking his target over and over. There's an energy swirling up, something so powerful I feel like I might break apart.

"Oh, Agkar," I moan again, and his hands find their way to my bouncing breasts. It feels as if his skin is burning up, or maybe it's mine. There's something happening in the space between us, like a rope is winding its way around me and pulling me closer and closer to him.

"Zirelle," he snarls, curling his tusks upward, "you must know now that you are mine."

He's right. The link between us is tightening around me

just as it's closing in around him, and it feels like we could very well merge into a single being.

"I do," I whimper. "I do know." Only Agkar could bring me to this place underneath the earth where only the two of us matter. For a moment, everything else fades into the background: Our jobs, our roles, our civilizations constantly trying to destroy one another. He is my orc, and I'm spread out before him, just as myself.

For the first time I feel like Zirelle, and not Captain Mastair.

"Good." His smile is tender yet dominating. "I'm going to fill you up. I'm going to put my seed so deep inside you that you will carry my whelps. You are mine."

The words are foreign to me, alien, and yet I want them. My mind is licking them, swirling them around, absorbing them deep into my chest.

"Yes!" I cry out. Suddenly nothing else matters except my orc, driving himself inside me, spilling himself where I can soak it all up. "Yes, give it to me. All of it." I want this world he's promising me more than anything, a world where it's just us.

There's a gravelly rumble in his throat as I feel him start to grow inside me, and he thrusts even faster, pushing me closer and closer toward my great explosion. I'm no longer just crying out now but screaming with each stroke, my eyes watering with my unspent orgasm. I clutch his hips, sucking him into me, bringing in everything he has to offer me. I want it all.

When Agkar bursts it's just what I need to leap, and I'm hurled into a madly-spinning whirlwind where we're together, completely together, our inner beings wrapped inextricably around one another. My thighs seize and my pussy clenches tight, and he's so huge that I can barely flex at all. I'm calling out his name as Agkar buries himself deep, as deep as he possibly can, and spills everything into me.

I finally have him, all of him. He's mine.

Gently, Agkar lowers my legs and falls to the bed on top of me. He draws one hand up to my face and it feels like his golden eyes are burrowing into my skin, seeking out what I am underneath. I know at that moment that he sees me—really sees me, past the sturdy wall I've built around myself, through the thick armor protecting me from the sharp edges of the world.

It is a marvelous thing to be seen, to be understood, to be embraced fully for what I am and not what I should be. When he kisses me, it's as if everything is right. My orc is where he belongs.

Then, all at once, it hits me what we've done.

CHAPTER 12

AGKAR

Everything I've been seeking, everything I've been missing, was there in front of me the whole time. My wonderful, irritating, beautiful captain. Out of everything that has happened to me, I expected her the least. But while I was swallowed to the hilt inside her, I could feel it—the bonding that was happening between us.

Mine. That is what she is: My human. My mate.

I make one last deep thrust inside her, imagining what her small body will do with the bounty I've given it. Will she swallow it all up, and in time, start to grow? I want to see her like that, heavy with my orcish brood. I want to see her breasts swell up and her nipples drip milk, and hold her in my lap as my whelp suckles her.

This is what it feels like, I think, to find the other half of your soul. To want only for their happiness, their companionship, their flawless body. I want to create a life with her, give her a safe home to live in, take away all the worry that has plagued her for who knows how long. I want to let her feel imperfect, and accept her anyway.

But after a moment, Zirelle's face no longer mimics mine. There is a slow horror finding its way into her eyes.

"Agkar," she says, so quiet I almost can't hear her. "What did we just do?"

I'm so surprised by her question that I don't answer right away. I feel more confused by it than anything. What could she mean? We're mated now, and I gave her every last drop of my seed. "What do you think?"

"We... We can't, um..." She fumbles for words. "There's no way that orcs and humans can, um, do that, right?"

It blindsides me. She doesn't know. Did she not understand what I was doing? What *we* were doing?

"Create offspring?" My voice is unsteady. "Yes, we can."

Her eyes go wide and her mouth falls slack. A drum inside my chest is beating harder and louder as she wriggles away from me. My cock falls out of her tight cunt so all of our combined juices seep out.

"No," she whispers. "That's not true."

What did she think was happening? I told her to her face, and she wanted it, too. She must feel it—the bond. She must understand the unbreakable connection that's now formed between us, and what it asks of us.

"It is true," I say. "I've seen it with my own eyes." It doesn't sting as much as I expect when I think of Nera, swollen up with another orc's child.

I try to pull Zirelle close to me, but she puts her hands on my chest and pushes me away.

"That can't be right." Her voice is husky, worried. I understand now that whatever she is feeling, it is not good.

"Isn't that what you wanted?" I ask. I don't understand.

She said the words. She felt the bond. She begged to have all of me inside her.

"I thought..." Zirelle looks like a horse ready to bolt. "I thought it was dirty talk."

My heart is hammering hard in my chest. How could she think that after the way we just joined? It was beyond lust this time. Surely she felt the twining of our inner bodies. She must know what's happened to us.

"Dirty talk?" I'm incredulous. "No, woman. I was quite serious. As I believed you were, too."

She drops her head into her hands, her breathing speeding up. I need to calm her down. She can't react this way, as if we've just made a grave mistake. Her eyes are squeezed closed, and ice is forming in my chest as she doesn't answer me.

I wrap my four-fingered hand around her arm and, as gently as I can, draw her towards me on the bed. "You felt it too, didn't you? The mating bond?" My gaze is focused intently on her as she finally looks up at me. "You must have."

"I don't know what you mean," she whispers.

"The new sense you have." I search for the right words. "Can't you feel that I'm here, but in a different way? A way you didn't know me before?"

"I..." Her voice is shaky. "I don't know what to think, Lieutenant."

The way she calls me by my title instead of my name makes me flinch.

"There is nothing to think about," I say, more firmly. "You're my mate. We'll have many whelps together. We'll get old together."

The crease between her brows is deepening. "But I'm human. I can't be—"

"That doesn't matter." I rub my thumbs in soothing circles on the backs of her hands. "Human or not, fate chose us."

She shakes her head furiously. "You must know that I can't do any of that." There's a heavy stone of dread settling in my belly. "I'm the captain of the guard, Lieutenant. You're my subordinate officer. We've broken so many rules already."

Zirelle can't really be turning me down, can she? There is no choice to be made. It's not something she can just decide to ignore.

"Then leave the guard," I say forcefully. "I can take care of you. I'll always take care of you." And I will. I would do anything to make sure she's safe and fed and happy.

"I don't need you to take care of me." Her tone is curt and stiff. "I have my job. I have my life. I can take care of myself."

I squash the ugly fear growing inside me. She just doesn't understand yet. She needs time to wrap her mind around it. Soon she'll feel how much she wants the same things I do.

"Yes, you can," I say instead. "You are capable, smart, and strong." Her shoulders relax as I tell her this. I need to be gentle, as if trying to tame a frightened animal. I can't have her run from me. "You must see what's happened, Zirelle."

But she is fighting it. While she knows I'm right, she's afraid of what it means for everything she's worked so hard to build.

"This isn't something we can do," she says firmly, almost firm enough to make me believe she feels it.

I close my eyes and focus on my breathing. I can't force her to acknowledge the truth. I'll have to let her come to me, in her own time.

The moment I think it, though, my heart constricts. She's mine now, and I would hope that I'm hers, too. To pretend otherwise feels wrong.

ZIRELLE

This must be some sort of practical joke. No, that mysterious force I felt as he was inside me was simply a manifestation of my lust and desire, spurred on by the way he kissed me, and sucked on me, and looked me in the eyes while he—

Fuck. I can't go down this path. I'm no one's mate. I know what this means to trollkin, living near them, watching their society. Even if we were *mates*, Agkar is my lieutenant and I'm his captain. If there was physical evidence, and I suddenly started growing round around the middle, that would just be the beginning of many uninvited questions.

I cover my face and breathe hard into my palms. This can't be happening. I don't want to even think about the sense of peace, the perfect rightness I felt as he stared down at me, his pulse thrumming through me...

Agkar's expression has opened to me now. I can see the orc underneath the hard demeanor and forceful *yes, sirs*—the orc with a hurt soul, and a brutal scar left on him from some woman I don't know.

The jealousy that strikes me is like the point of a knife. He was in love with someone before me. He cared for her enough that he left his post and came here to the desert just to escape her. Is that what this is about? Did he claim me because he wishes he had claimed her, instead? Does she still own that part of his heart?

Now, suddenly, I want to take it from her. I want to own all of him.

"What was her name?" I ask. I don't know why, but at this very moment, I need to know the truth. The ferocity of my question makes Agkar furrow his brow. We were talking about something else, but I can't remember what it was.

"Whose name?" he asks, perplexed.

"The other human." My words come out laced with venom. I don't know what's taken over me, but I feel fierce and clawed.

Agkar studies me. "Nera. That was her name."

I turn it over in my mind. Nera. Did he kiss me thinking of her? Did he lick me wishing I were her? Did he fill me up imagining her instead? I cannot tolerate this idea.

"Do you think of Nera now?" I ask him, forcefully.

His muscles are tensing. I feel like he's looking inside of me. Eventually, he shakes his head and says, "No."

The relief is like that soothing salve in his med kit. "Good." But I don't know what to make of it, this furious envy that's taken over me.

There is a spark of understanding in his eyes, and he uses his other arm to draw me closer to him. I should fight, keep my distance until we figure this out, but I would rather do anything else.

"There is no one," he says, quieter and softer than I've ever heard him before. "There is no one in my heart but you, Zirelle."

His words settle this irrational, angry part of me, but they ask many other questions. I'm frightened that he feels for me so deeply—and that I feel the same for him. I can't ignore the truth that I am seeing him differently. I can feel his presence near me, not as a warm body, but more like an essence, and it's already melded with mine. That, I know, can't be undone.

I've made a grave mistake tonight by letting him in. I couldn't have known it would lead to this, but now I regret ever opening the door. I want nothing more than to lie like this next to him every night for the rest of my life. As fiercely as I protest, the idea of sharing that with Agkar brings a little bird to life in my chest. That would be a good existence, I think, to love my orc.

But it's impossible. There is no space for him, no place he

can readily fit inside what I've already built, and I must defend this fortress with my life.

AGKAR

She is jealous.

This is a very encouraging sign. Zirelle is feeling the effects of our mating, our souls bonding to one another, and it is hitting her hard and fast.

I've heard stories about moments like these, when it begins. Fierce fighting, and even fiercer rutting. Sometimes a trollkin's emotions become too powerful to control. Who knows what it's like for a human?

Luckily, Zirelle seems satisfied by my answer that I am not thinking of Nera. No, I'm not thinking of anything but my captain, every last flawless curve of her, and how I already want to devour her again. I want to make her mine over and over, ensuring she's filled to the brim until my dying day.

It's hitting me, too. The agony I felt as she rejected me is unparalleled. But I can't let it control me—I can't let it dictate how I treat her. It will only scare her away, someone as independent as my captain.

But as I lie next to her and she slowly drifts off into sleep, I can't help feeling that everything is right. This is how it was always supposed to be. Nera was just a step on the ladder towards finding Zirelle, my human, my everything.

Finally, I do fade into dreams, my arms wrapped tightly around her, wondering what will come tomorrow.

It arrives too soon. I wake up at dawn, my stomach knotted. I should be at peace sleeping next to my mate, but the world beyond this room fills me with anxiety. Zirelle is still dreaming, her eyes twitching under her closed lids. Then she jolts awake. At first, a soft smile spreads across her face, as if she's glad to see me here beside her—until the weight of the world settles on her mind, and the smile fades.

"You should get back to the barracks," Zirelle says quietly, as if she's afraid of disturbing the silence. "Before anyone notices you're gone."

Right. Of course. As much as I don't want to leave her, we have duties to attend to, and I don't need to be stirring up suspicion by getting caught leaving her house. I close my eyes, trying to put what happened last night out of my mind, then get out of bed.

Once I have my clothes back on, Zirelle sits up. "Don't be late to your shift." She tries to make the air lighter between us, as if last night wasn't as serious as it was.

But I cannot pretend any longer. My life is irrevocably changed, and it all hinges on whether or not she can accept the same.

"I'm never late," is all I say. Then I head for the door and let myself out.

CHAPTER 13

ZIRELLE

I feel strangely alone when he's gone, the morning sun spilling in the window. But I have duties to attend to, just as I do every day.

I focus on my to-do list. I don't have a reason to see the lieutenant today, and I hope that our paths won't cross by accident. He finally showed himself to me, and I responded by placing a solid wall between us. My guilt rises up like bile.

Isn't this what I wanted? To finally connect as individuals, as lovers, and not just as captain and lieutenant?

No, not like this. I have too many responsibilities to even consider whatever Agkar's offering. Keeping the claws of the drink off of me and trying to care for the needs of the city is already more than I can handle.

It turns out I have bigger things to worry about anyway. There's a hearing scheduled for the one remaining member of the Black Fox. He was identified as Forsten Heed, a man often seen around the local watering hole. He must have been casing the Black Fox's targets for them. He associated with other humans and trollkin alike, and often worked as a go-between for the two sides in trade transactions.

But the morning of the hearing, we find him dead in his jail cell, with the cell guard unconscious outside.

"I think it's clear that someone didn't want him to talk," I tell my assembled officers—which includes Lieutenant Agkar, of course. He looks straight ahead, at attention. "That means Heed knew something important. We need to find out what that was, and who wanted it to be kept a secret."

Our first order of business is to drum up everyone who knew him, and piece together a picture of what the Black Fox might have been doing to get their one remaining member whacked. And it'll be up to me and the lieutenant to question them—one human and one trollkin, so we won't look biased.

"Start at the east side tavern," Corporal Jar'kel tells us. "I'll begin in the merchant quarter."

Every head in the watering hole turns when the lieutenant and I walk in together. We start with the bartender, an old orc with a big scar across his face, and he's thankfully cooperative. Most of the everyday people who work in Attirex know the drill when it comes to dealing with the city guard.

"There are a few new, unsavory types in town," the bartender tells us. "I saw Heed meet with at least one of them last time he was here."

Agkar and I exchange a glance. Our first interview yields a solid lead. Maybe the Black Fox was in business with someone new, and that someone didn't want their identity to get out.

"Point them out to me," I say. Just then, the door opens and a familiar purple-blue troll walks in.

Lo'zar.

The bartender nods at him. "That guy. Just showed up last week. Comes in here frequently. Not sure what his business is."

I thank him for the information, but the last thing I want to do is interrogate the troll I took home with me one random night. Especially not with the lieutenant right next to me.

"Let's pull him aside," Agkar says, nodding at Lo'zar. I can't avoid it. I have no reason to refuse.

We corner him at the same seat by the window where I had picked him up just a few nights ago. His eyes go wide when he sees me, and a huge smile crosses his face.

"Ah, it's you," he says, eyes twinkling. Then he takes in my uniform, and the smile dims. "And who are you playing as today?"

Agkar looks between us, perplexed by our familiarity.

"I'm Captain Mastair," I tell him. "Of the Attirex city guard."

"Oh." Lo'zar clearly didn't know that's who had taken him home, because I didn't want him to know—for this very reason. "I didn't realize."

"Have you met the captain before?" Agkar asks, eyes sliding between us.

Lo'zar chuckles at the question. "Have I?" He glances at me, then winks. "Never. Not once."

But none of this escapes my lieutenant's notice. His lip curls up on one side.

This will not be good.

AGKAR

Could this be him? The male that my little human took to bed with her—could it really be this big, ugly troll? I'm horrified and enraged by the idea of this brute with his big, jagged tusks putting his hands all over my Zirelle. I want to take his head and twist it off his body, then crush it like a melon.

"What's your name?" Captain Mastair asks, but I can tell by the tone of the question that she already knows the answer.

The troll studies us, and the humor on his face when he first saw the captain has all faded. "It's Lo'zar," he says. "What's this about, *Captain*?"

I curl my hands into fists at my side to keep them from leaping across the table and choking him as I imagine him curling those jeweled fingers around her ass. Did he kiss her when I hadn't taken the chance, and tasted her before I could? Did she come all over his cock, too?

My rage is a red cloud creeping in on the edges of my vision.

"We're investigating something," the captain says. "A recent crime."

Lo'zar holds up both hands in surrender. "I'm not involved in anything like that. Clean as a whistle."

"That sure sounds guilty," I growl. "When no one's accused you of anything yet."

The captain shoots me a glare. This is her interrogation, not mine. But suddenly I want nothing more than to chew this troll with his big, idiot tusks into little bits. He's most likely a low-level henchman, sent to do somebody else's job who's higher up the food chain. If this were back home, in Gagzen, I could simply string him up and torture him until he told me what I wanted to know.

"Lieutenant," Captain Mastair says in warning, but her eyes are guilty, and that tells me everything I need to know. I'm right.

I manage to keep myself restrained, but inside I'm roiling, ready to overflow. Why did she do it? I can't stop picturing someone else's hands on her, running up and down her sides, playing with her breasts.

She turns back to the troll. "We're actually asking about a man named Forsten. Forsten Heed?"

"Heed?" He tilts his head, surprised. "That guy? Oh, he tried to sell me some goods. I had a feeling it was stolen. Just smelled hot, you know? He asked a bunch of people to buy, like he was trying to get rid of it quick."

"Maybe you're not as stupid as you look," I grumble, and the captain elbows me in the side. Lucky for her, there's nothing but muscle there.

The troll scowls.

"Quick?" Captain Mastair asks. "What did he try to sell you?"

He looks between us, and wrinkles up his nose like what he's about to say is against his better nature. Then he sizes up the captain again, and leans in towards her. I want to just reach out and strangle him. "The green salt," he says, as if just for her ears.

The same stuff my soldiers and I consumed from time to time when we wanted to forget about war for a few hours, but in its crystallized form. So the Black Fox was also dealing in more illicit trades. Or at least, Forsten Heed was. The kind of people who deal in the green are the same type of people who might kill someone to keep them from talking.

The captain frowns thoughtfully, making the same connection. "Is there anything else you could tell us about this guy, Lo'zar?" the captain asks, and I despise that she's using his name in such a familiar way. How many times did she see him? The boiling inside me is almost to its breaking point.

He leans his head on one hand. "As I said, I haven't been here long. I didn't know him."

The captain nods, and I can't tell if she believes him or not.

She's good at disguising herself, hiding what she's really thinking and feeling. "Thanks for the information." We get up from the table. The troll offers her a hand, and she shakes it. When he offers it to me I glare at him with the full weight of my hatred, and taken aback, he leans away.

"All right, then," he says, and waves as he heads off to the bar.

Once we're outside, Captain Mastair turns on me.

"What was that?" she demands. "Getting all up in his face? Interrupting my questioning?"

"You fucked him, didn't you?" I snarl back. Her mouth falls open. For a second, her disguise falls, and I know that I'm right. "I thought so."

I had hoped I was wrong, but I knew. I want to turn back around and slam that damned troll's head into the bar top.

She squares her shoulders. "And what business is it of yours, Lieutenant?" she hisses.

How could she ask me such a thing after what we did? My fury has become a volcano. "Because you are *mine*!" I grab her by the arm and pull her away from the bar, into an alleyway. I push her up against the wall and her eyes are wide and her mouth is round. All I want to do is press my lips against it, to see it wrapped around my cock again. But then I see his cock instead, and the rage returns tenfold. "You are mine, Zirelle. Why you would ever go to a cretin like that..."

"How dare you." She pulls her arm back and rubs it where I've grabbed her. "I can do what I like. Anyway"—she narrows her eyes and scowls at me—"I have needs. It's not like you were banging down my door."

I growl at this. "Didn't I?" I lean in close, my body towering over hers, and I can hear when her breath catches in her throat. I know immediately when she feels what I feel—the thirst. The hunger.

The captain tentatively nods her head. "You knocked. Lightly."

I prop myself against the wall with one arm and lean down as far as I can, so I'm breathing against her sensitive ears. "Why him?" She lets out a gasp as my lips travel over her earlobe. "Did you fuck him because what you really wanted was me, instead?" All I want to do is tear her clothes off right here. It's a quiet alley, and I would be quick about it.

"Lieutenant." Her breath is coming faster as my hands make their way around her waist. Her hips unconsciously lean into me. "W-what an inappropriate question."

My mouth travels further down to her throat, where I drag my tusks over her skin. Her back arches against me. "I'm full of those," I say. "Tell me. Did you want me, and that's why you took him home with you?" I stop at her collar and nip at her skin, then smooth it over with my lips.

"Yes." Her voice is husky.

"And now?" I ask, running my fingers up underneath her captain's coat. She's shivering. "Now that you have me, will you ever think of him again?"

I drop my hands to her hips and run them over her pants, knowing she's imagining me taking them off of her.

"No," she whispers.

"Good." I cup her ass hard and tight, and Zirelle moans against my neck. I want to ravage her right here. Every last one of my instincts is telling me to grab her and jam myself into her as hard as I can, fill her up and claim her again and again.

I take a few deep breaths. No. I need to wait. She must come to understand the bond in her own time, what it means, what it demands of her. This joining between us has to be accepted and welcomed in her own way or else we will both suffer.

I pull away from her, and she lets out a little irritated noise.

"We'd better not get caught," I say. She is clearly still wanting, but I won't let her have it—not yet.

The captain knows I'm right, so she straightens up and adjusts her coat. She shoots me a glare. "We had better start looking for green salt traders," she says.

I smirk. I love when she gets bossy. "Lead the way."

CHAPTER 14

ZIRELLE

It's difficult to think of anything else except Agkar's cock pressed against my hips as we continue our investigation.

The green salt has been the bane of my existence since I was first promoted to captain. It's always moving underneath Attirex, and every day we find at least one human or trollkin dead in an alleyway after breathing in too much of it. It's easy to do, I hear, when the green takes hold of you, because you just want more and more.

"So, the Black Fox was dealing in salt, too?" Corporal Jar'kel asks. He's been following up on other leads on the eastern end of the city. "I thought we curbed this when we squashed the Hookclaws."

"Maybe it's someone new," I suggest.

"We should crack down on search and seizure." Jar'kel looks irritated. "Maybe they're funneling it inside of some other goods."

"Or they're using the tunnels again," I say. "We should check them and clear them out."

He grunts. "Good idea, Captain." Before he leaves my office, he stops in the doorway. "Is there something else going on I should know about?"

A wave of dread washes over me. "I'm not sure what you're asking, Corporal."

He looks at me for a long moment, then shakes his head and leaves my office without another word.

Do I carry some sort of stink on me? Can he sense that something has happened between the lieutenant and me?

I can't let Jar'kel get wind of this. He may respect my authority, but I don't know what he would do if he found out. It could cost me my job.

That night, I'm not surprised when I hear a knock at my door. Agkar stands on the other side, his eyes pure liquid with desire after our interrogation and subsequent encounter in the alleyway. I want him just as much. He would probably take me the way he took me last night, appreciating every inch of me, making me scream while our souls wrap around each other.

Damn.

"It's you," I say, rather stupidly. He takes a step towards me, but I don't move to let him in.

"It's me," he agrees. But my trepidation must show on my face, because Agkar's open expression turns darker. "Won't you invite me in?"

My hands are trembling. I don't want to turn him away, but I don't have a choice, either. This thing happening between us can't happen. I can't give him what he wants.

It's kinder to stop this now, before it gets even worse.

"Agkar..." I begin, and the tone of my voice makes him tense up. "We can't do this."

"Can't do what?" He takes another step towards me, so my

chin is at his chest level, and he's looking down at me. "I know you want me inside you. Wrapped around you. Holding you. Right now."

I do. I want that more than anything. But I have to shut this down before it can get out of hand. "I can't be your mate, Agkar."

His face turns hard and unyielding. He hooks a hand under my chin and tilts my head up so I'm looking at him, and when I try to draw back, he won't let me go.

"You can't mean that." His mouth is pressed in a hard line, but his gold eyes are wide and vulnerable, hurt and pleading. "You don't mean that, Zirelle."

"It's better for both of us," I say. "It would never work out, you know that. There's no future here."

"I know you feel what I feel," he says, keeping his voice calm and firm. "We're bound together now, and that bond doesn't care about futures."

I cross my arms because it's the only way I can hold myself back from returning his touch. "Well, it will have to."

"It will still pull us together." He shakes his head. "You can't deny it."

"I will deny it." But as I say it, I feel the words clamming up in my mouth, and a pressure builds behind my eyes.

There's a deep frustration on his face. "Please," Agkar says, and he reaches out to take my hand in his. Our fingers brush, and then I pull mine away. I can't give an inch or else I'll give a mile, and then I'll let him into my house and wrap my legs around his hips and take all of him inside me. "Don't fight it, Zirelle." His eyes are sad. "It will hurt. I don't want that for you."

"This is the way things have to be, Agkar. As much as I wish it were different, as much as I wish you could stay, I can't jeopardize my life here." It's all I have. It's all I've ever had. "I'm sorry."

His face slackens, and I know I've injured him. I will leave another scar on his heart, even bigger than Nera's. He told me he was mine, that I was his. He did not give that up to me easily.

Without another word, Agkar turns around and walks away, back toward the barracks. His shoulders are tight and drawn, and his hands are clenched into fists at his sides.

I can't stand watching him go, but I have to.

AGKAR

She's turned me away in no uncertain terms, and there's nothing I can do about it. I could try to force her to understand, but it would only harden her even more against me. No. All I can do is wait. Her need for me will grow so great that she won't be able to stay away.

Of course I understand the position that she's in. The city guard is all she's ever known, and her role is of paramount importance to her. It's her legacy. But my Zirelle will know soon that this is greater than even that.

When I return to my room in the barracks, I can think of nothing but her face, her voice, and her bottomless dark eyes. I picture how cutely she scowls when I don't do what she wants, and my heart starts to race. I stroke my hard cock, remembering how right it felt to hold her in my arms and fall asleep beside her, and soon I'm exploding all over my hand. Then, when the need grows too great, I shoot one off again. I wonder how many nights I'll have to do this before she comes to her senses. I hope it's not many, but my captain is stubborn and I'm not sure if I'll be able to outlast her.

The next day, she chooses a small team to raid the underground tunnels that doesn't include me, and it takes everything in my power to quell my rage. She's trying to keep us apart so that she doesn't have to face me. I suppose that I can't fault her for that, because not seeing her is the only thing keeping my own ravenous desires at bay.

Unfortunately, the raid turns up nothing of interest—just a few petty criminals already living on the edges. Wherever the green salt is coming from, it's through more clever means. There is no resolution for the murdered member of the Black Fox. Whoever's salt he was peddling, we can't find a trace of its source.

My captain is beyond enraged. After only a few weeks with no new leads, the power of her unsatisfied need is beginning to weigh on her. Her brow is always creased, her mouth screwed up into a scowl. She becomes short and ill-tempered. She bosses all of us around even more than before, and she latches onto any failure with the quickness of a predator.

"Lieutenant," she says over my shoulder one afternoon. I turn around and try to keep my gaze steady and even, though her presence sends a sharp and insistent bolt of desire through my chest.

"Yes, Captain?" I keep my tone deferential.

"Tax revenues are down. Are you failing to report shipments?"

It's such a direct accusation that I'm surprised. Usually she's fairer than this. "We're running the same operation as before," I answer, remaining calm. "Everything that passes through is assessed and taxed."

"Then someone is smuggling the expensive goods right under your nose." Her dark eyebrows are tense. "This time of year, revenue should be climbing. You're missing something, Lieutenant."

All I want to do is throw her down on the searching table and fuck her, to ease this terrible tension inside both of us, but I keep my voice steady as I say, "I'll pay closer attention, Captain."

She nods curtly, not looking me in the eyes. "Good."

Every interaction between us is like this one—short, businesslike, matter-of-fact. Soon I can feel her presence whenever she's nearby, even if she's not in the same room. It's like a beacon of light moving about, tormenting me, calling my name and turning me away at the same time.

I wish she wouldn't do this, keeping us from what we both know we need. What do I have to do to make her see the truth? To realize everything else doesn't matter?

My misery is a boulder strapped to my back as our leads on the green salt dry up. There's more and more of it coming into the city, so we crack down on search and seizures. We check every single shipment that moves through Attirex, much to our displeasure and that of the merchants. Wait times increase, and our work never seems to end. But the number of salt deaths climbs upward, and as weeks become months, there is mounting pressure on the city guard to find out where it's coming from and then stop it.

Zirelle is not handling it well. There's a drawn look to her face, and she's always impatiently drumming her fingers on whatever she can find—her desk, her knee, her dagger. That's how I know she hasn't gone elsewhere to have her pleasures sated, or returned to the troll in the tavern, because she knows nothing will fill her up the way I do. I can't smell alcohol on her, either, which I take to mean she has not fallen back on the drink to drown her miseries. That's good, at least. If she did, I would be forced to act.

I'm not faring so well myself. She is in my thoughts every moment, and her absence from my arms and my bed is a bottomless, gaping hole. It drags on and on, every day aching worse than the previous day, and I want nothing more than to wrap up my captain tight and solve this problem for her. Except not even Corporal Jar'kel can drum up a lead, and every new start stops at a dead-end.

It's when I see that her captain's jacket isn't fitting her the same way it used to that I start to grow concerned. Zirelle's chest seems bigger, more pronounced, and the jacket doesn't close fully over her hips. Her gait has changed, too, and it almost looks like something hurts.

Is she eating properly? Getting exercise? Or am I haunting her dreams the same way that she haunts mine?

She spends more time in her office as the needs of the city pile up higher. The captain's failure is building up until it looks like it's crushing her.

I know then that she needs me. Whether or not she'll even let me inside her house, she needs me. So that night, I go to her front door and knock.

I hear shuffling on the other side. After a few more moments, the knob turns and the door opens.

Zirelle is not pleased to see me. "I told you that you couldn't come here." Her eyes are piercing. It's clear that she does not want to have to turn me away again.

"It will be a brief visit." I nod at her. "I just need a few minutes."

After considering, she steps aside lets me in with a wary eye.

"Why are you wearing your coat?" I ask, not moving to sit down. I simply stand in the doorway, watching her busy around, moving an object from one place to another as if she's tidying up.

"Why not?" She huffs and puts down a candleholder. "It's my house."

It's quite hot tonight as we drift closer to summer, and there's no reason to be wearing such a big heavy thing at home. I take a step toward her, and she freezes in place. I inhale the air, and all I get is the tang of her. She wants me. She wants me, but she won't let herself have me.

Gently, I take the shoulders of the coat in my hands, and push them down her arms.

"Lieutenant..." She doesn't try to stop me, but her face changes from annoyance to fear. I'm not undressing her, and I try to make that clear in the ginger way that I pull the sleeves from her hands and then toss the garment onto the floor.

Her breasts are bigger. And her belly—it's more rounded than before, noticeably so.

My blood starts to pump faster. There's a ringing sound in my ears.

"Zirelle," I say carefully. "Were you ever going to tell me?"

CHAPTER 15

ZIRELLE

He's found me out.

I started feeling sick early on. That was what told me that something was wrong. But I kept it under wraps, only throwing up in my private outhouse. A few times I was caught by surprise and made an excuse to puke in an alleyway, but so far, no one has acted at all suspicious about it.

I thought at first I was just torn up, that keeping myself away from Agkar was taking its toll on me. I couldn't get him out of my mind. I was consumed with the thought of him, of his hands on my skin, his mouth on mine. Every time I saw him and couldn't have him was like a blow with a blunted weapon.

But when my periods stopped coming, and my belly started growing thicker, I knew.

How long could I hide it and get away with not answering questions? Many members of the city guard have families, naturally. But I'm the captain, and a woman, no less. It's different for me. If I don't leave my post, who will raise my child for me? And what happens when that child inevitably emerges half orc and half human?

With the investigation into the green salt going so poorly, I can't spend any of my mental energy on questions like that. I have a job to do, and I'm going to do it. Perhaps I can somehow still keep my position if I just find the source and destroy it. Certainly no one could question my value then.

I knew Agkar would find out sooner or later, but it's still the last thing I wanted to happen. It's the last thing I need, on top of everything else, and still my body is inching towards him like a magnet. I want nothing more than to have his arms around me again, to taste his lips again, to feel his hands everywhere. I want, I want, I want...

How am I so weak for this orc? I have never felt the pull to be close to someone like I do now. I long more than anything for our inner selves to twine around each other like mating snakes in the desert.

"Why didn't you tell me?" he asks, extending his hand like he's about to touch me, then he stops himself. I have to look away from his face because it's almost too much. I've hurt Agkar, just as I've hurt myself by keeping this secret from him.

"I don't know," I finally say. "What good would it have done, if I told you?" Neither of us can change it now. It's my problem to deal with and figure out, just as the needs of the city are.

He raises his hand again and this time, it settles on my shoulder. He takes a step towards me and I can suddenly feel him all around me, in that way where I'm not feeling his body, but his essence. The smell of him is almost overpowering in its familiarity. All I want is to fall into him, to lean on him and give my tired soul a rest, but I must resist.

If it's been this difficult already to survive, to stay away, I can't imagine how the remainder of my pregnancy will be.

"Zirelle," my orc says, letting his other hand drop to my waist. He leans down just enough that he can look right into my eyes. "You don't have to do this by yourself."

"Yes, I do." Doesn't he get it? We don't get to raise a little family together, as much as I want it. As much as I want *him*. There is no happily ever after for us.

Rather than arguing with me, Agkar lets out a deep sigh and draws me into him, and my burning need for comfort and affection is so great that I tip forward and fall. When he crushes me against his body, all my misery and loneliness swells up to the surface. His touch is like the warmest, softest bed, and the sobs break out of me before I can stop them.

"I'm sorry," I say, burying my face in his chest. "I didn't know how to tell you. I didn't want to. I wanted to pretend that this had never happened." My legs give out from the force of my emotions, and Agkar catches me easily.

"But you can't anymore, can you?" he asks. Sliding one arm under my knees, he picks me up and carries me back to my bed.

I just shake my head. This has all gone so terribly, terribly wrong.

AGKAR

My poor Zirelle. Part of me is angry at her for keeping me in the dark, but I know why she did. Everything she knows is crumbling around her, all while she's forcing herself to keep me at arm's length. I could have been there to soothe her, instead. I wish she would allow herself to lean on me, instead of shouldering every burden alone. But she has lived so long fighting her own fights that she feels she has no choice.

I carry her to her bed and sit down, bringing her into my lap the way I might a child. The tears flow fast and hot from her eyes, and her body shudders with every sob. I am surprised that my stern, hard captain has come undone in my arms, but I have heard that orcesses and trollesses can get quite emotional while they are carrying whelps. Human women must be the same.

I am overwhelmed as I watch her break down this way, but I keep it carefully locked up inside, choosing instead to gently stroke her hair and let her cry. As the tears stream down her face, a fierce and fiery protectiveness starts to rise up inside me. She doesn't need this burden on top of everything else. I will topple and conquer anything that makes my Zirelle feel this way. I will destroy and stomp on the ashes of whatever might put our family in danger—or keep me from them again.

I'm saddened, too, that our whelp is such an awful and dreaded thing. When I thought of what this moment would be like, I imagined it would be much happier: The beginning of something beautiful, not the end of it.

Zirelle sobs until there's not a single tear left inside her, and then she lies against me, silent. I can hear the thrumming of her heart in my own chest, beating in synchronicity with mine. I draw my hand down her shoulder to her belly, and let it rest on the soft swell there. She flinches at first, but doesn't move away.

"It is an incredible thing, isn't it?" I ask. "That we could create life." Despite everything, I am amazed by it. Despite everything, there is a small bastion of hope inside me now.

Her answer is so quiet I almost can't hear it. "It's a wonder. I wish I could appreciate that."

"I know this is not what you wanted to happen," I say,

running my hands along her soft body. "But now it has, and I don't want you to feel you are alone."

Zirelle turns her face towards me and her eyes are red with tears. I bring her in as tight as I possibly can to show her I can support her weight. "I don't have a choice," she says.

"There are always choices." I could simply swallow her up, keeping her safe and secured like this until it's time. Then, I want to keep cradling her in the nest of my lap while she holds our whelp close. "There is a whole wide world out there of possibilities."

I understand, of course, what it means to have always been a soldier, and to see yourself as a soldier until the day you die. But suddenly, this person in front of me—she fills up my entire vision until I can't make out anything but her. Everything else seems extraneous.

"You don't understand," she whispers. "This is all I am. It's all I've ever been, and all I ever will be. It's my duty, my responsibility. It's... it's all I have left of them."

Her parents. She's afraid of losing the one thing she's dedicated her entire life to. How can I possibly free her from that prison?

"What if I left?" I ask.

She stills in my arms. "What do you mean?"

"A resignation." It would be dishonorable, but now that feels more than worthwhile.

She looks up at me, and her expression is worried. "Lieutenant?" She corrects herself. "Agkar? Why? Why would you do that?"

"So that you don't have to!" I don't mean to say it so loudly, but I'm frustrated and angry. If this is what it takes for us to be together, to raise this whelp together, then I'll do it. I can't let Zirelle slip out of my arms. I can't lose her, and I can't lose our family—not when this is all I've ever wanted, and I simply didn't realize it before.

She's quiet for a long time, thinking. I feel her relax into me, and when I run my hand down to her belly, she lets me.

"You would do that?" she asks, barely audible.

I burrow my face into her perfect hair. She smells like everything I've needed, like the missing piece of my heart. "I would do anything."

ZIRELLE

He would give it all up? It's ludicrous. Beyond outlandish.

"You can't," I say. "Your job is everything to you. I don't know anyone more dedicated." And it's true. Agkar has become my most hardworking officer. He does what I say without question now, quickly and efficiently and intelligently.

"I can." He sighs against me. "I will do whatever I have to."

The affection I feel for him at that moment is overwhelming. He would give everything up for me and this child of ours? It's touching and sad, and ultimately pointless.

"It doesn't matter," I say. We can't be together anyway, even if he did all that. "Once anyone knew, it wouldn't matter if you were still in the guard or not. They would be..." I wrinkle up my nose. "They would be disgusted with me. I wouldn't survive it."

Agkar doesn't respond for a long moment. I tilt my head up to get a good look at his face, and he's staring right back at me. "We have done nothing wrong," he says, hand traveling over my belly. "You are perfect, and this little one is, too."

For just a moment, with the three of us together, I can imagine a different life: A life where every day isn't a desperate struggle to stay afloat, treading water only to keep drowning. A life where this child is my hope for the future rather than my curse. I have to hold in more tears as I imagine that sort of freedom.

"Zirelle." He fervently kisses my forehead. "Anything is possible. Our destiny belongs to us."

I want to believe him so badly, but wouldn't it be a betrayal of everything I've worked for? Everything my parents died for? I can't let them down that way. I bury my face deeper in his strong chest, drawn to the smell of him, encased in the raw power of his embrace.

I don't know which of us initiates it, but soon his lips are on mine, and my hands are wrapped around his neck. There's a franticness to his kisses that I give back tenfold, because all I want is him. It's what I've been craving for months and my need is limitless. I have no more willpower to resist, and I desire nothing more than to let go and have him catch me.

Neither of us has the fortitude to wait now, and our clothes are off in moments. Once my chest is exposed, Agkar goes right to devouring each of my tender nipples, his tusks dragging against my skin. He's sweating in the hot night air and it beads over his defined pectorals, sliding down his carved abdomen. His cock is already powerfully hard for me, jutting out in front of him proudly.

All I want is to have him inside me.

"Please," I say, my voice trembling. Agkar's sharp features soften for me and he leans forward, running one hand from my breast to my rounded belly, then down to the hot, dripping place between my legs. He tests me with his fingers tenderly, getting me ready. Then, once he's crouched over me, his face only inches away from mine, he slides in with a pristine gentleness. I moan as my body happily welcomes him in. My orc fills me until I can't take anymore, and then he starts to thrust deep, rocking back and forth inside me as our bodies finally reunite.

"I'm yours," Agkar whispers, his green-gold eyes staring into my soul.

"You're mine," I repeat, gasping as he fills me up again. "And I'm yours."

"You're mine," he agrees. I clutch him as close as I can, and he holds me fast as he loves me with his entire body.

"You feel incredible," he groans. "You are everything."

I run my hands up his chest to his tusks, then around his neck, wanting to memorize every last inch of him. Soon the sensation becomes almost too much to bear, and he holds me even tighter, rooting me to the earth.

"I'm there," I whisper into his neck, hoarse.

He thrusts faster, his warm breath tickling my face, his body filling mine to the brim with every wonderful thing he is. "Give it all to me."

That's when it takes me. I feel like nothing could top this, not ever. I bury my face in Agkar's neck as he, too, steps off the cliff with me. Tears work their way into my eyes again, my body too overwhelmed to hold them back. Will I always be a puddle of emotions like this?

"My Zirelle." He cradles my head, kissing my hair. "I won't ever let you go."

Of course, I know who Agkar really is: My mate, through and through. And I can't keep living without him.

CHAPTER 16

AGKAR

It is almost impossible to leave her early that morning, but I manage to get out of bed and put my clothes back on before the sun comes up. Zirelle is still asleep, breathing gentle puffs of air. I kiss her forehead, then run my hands over the swell of her belly where our whelp is curled up tight inside.

I don't know what comes next, but I will do anything for her and this small creature we've made.

While I get cleaned up, I turn over the night in my mind. It all feels like such an impossible problem, where no matter what, we lose something. We can't keep what we're doing hidden forever, but once it gets out... I think of Zirelle, full and heavy and still trying to cover up our secret, and my frustration roars to the surface. There has to be a way out of this, a path where I can be with my woman and watch our whelp grow up.

That day I decide to oversee inspections out at the front

gates, just to avoid catching a glimpse of her. If I did, I don't know that I'd be able to control myself.

People are impatient as guards search every last one of their belongings. There are merchant caravans, families, individuals with only a pack over one shoulder. For hours I watch humans and trollkin alike come and go, breathless from their trip across the desert, or holding their breath as they embark back into it. Each pregnant woman who walks past looks like Zirelle. I'm consumed with the thought of her, and I wonder if that will ever change again.

Most of the women who come through, human and trollkin alike, are all by themselves. I imagine them walking across the desert with just what they have in their packs or their carts. Where are the fathers, letting their mates and unborn offspring go alone? Most of the women look frightened, ready to bolt at the sound of a gunshot.

My gut twists when I think of Zirelle and my own whelp, wandering the hot sands without me.

Something about the image of her triggers a thought. The green salt is getting in right under our noses, even though we've searched every material possession entering the city. I pause as yet another lone human woman arrives, round with child. The cart is searched, and nothing is seized. The most noticeable thing about her is her walk—she doesn't have that same odd gait that Zirelle has developed.

I step out into the road where a guard is about to let her pass and stop him. The human woman is watching me with fear.

"We're going to inspect you," I tell her in my very limited Freysian. The woman's eyes widen, and I turn to one of the human guards. "Not me," I tell him. "You will."

"Inspect *her*, sir?" he asks. He does not look pleased, but I'm his superior officer, and he'll do what I ask.

The guard steps out cautiously and starts to pat her down, beginning at her shoulders and working his way to her legs. Little gasps travel down the line of people waiting to enter the city as they watch this novel occurrence. The guard pauses at her big belly, like he's afraid of touching her there. It's an understandable hesitation, but this is what I'm most interested in examining.

"Don't be a coward," I snap, and he gives me an accusatory glare as he starts to examine it. But after a moment he pauses, and his hand suddenly grabs her shirt. The woman jumps back to flee, but he stops her and calls me over.

Sure enough, there is no pregnant belly underneath—instead we find two great big bags of the green salt packed in tight. The woman is sobbing, and the guard translates for me. She was forced into this, she claims, on penalty of death. Her children are being held hostage.

I bring her in for questioning and call for the captain right away.

ZIRELLE

Agkar is panting when he enters my office.

"We found it," he says. "How the salt is getting into the city. We found it."

When he explains the woman at the city gate, it all starts to make sense. I want to hug him and kiss him and even more than that, but I resist and say, "Good work, Lieutenant."

We bring the woman in for questioning, and it's hard for her to talk through her terrified tears. Eventually I make all the trollkin leave the room because their presence is obviously making things worse, and I kneel down in front of her.

"You have to tell me who made you do this," I say. "So we can stop them."

She sniffles and wipes snot away from her face. "A trolkin," she says, holding in her sob. "She's holding my children, and she'll kill them if I fail. I can't fail!"

Viscerally I understand her panic, her need to do whatever she has to in order to keep her children safe. I try to comfort her as best I can.

"If you can show me where to find her, we can stop her, and get your children out. But you have to help me do that. Okay?"

The woman nods rapidly, even more tears streaming down her cheeks. I pat her on the shoulder and step back. It's time to move.

I inform the rest of the guard what we've discovered. We have a new mission now: The woman was kidnapped in a village about thirty miles away, near a small oasis that's almost dried up. Our culprit must be nearby.

"How do we lure out our perp?" Corporal Jar'kel asks. "They must be in hiding."

I smile broadly. "Me."

Agkar immediately objects. "That would put you in danger! What if she finds out who you are?"

I know why he's opposing my plan, and I need him to back off or risk exposing us. "Lieutenant. This is my decision. Now everyone, let's move out."

Agkar's jaw clenches and flexes, but he doesn't say anything else. He knows better. I'm the only one in the target demographic. I'm the perfect bait.

Armed with a wagon full of basic supplies and a bundle that looks like a baby in my arms, we leave for the village where the woman told us she was abducted. I'll make myself look as vulnerable as possible, and the moment I'm nabbed, I've commanded the guard to move.

It's almost a day of travel to reach the little town of Maizel. As we approach, the guard abandons me, my single horse, and the fake bundle of baby in my arms so it looks like I'm entering the village alone. My team is watching from behind buildings and on rooftops as I walk to the center of town, pretending to be exhausted and miserable. I buy some water, making a show of using my last few coins, and even trade a few of the essential goods in my cart just to really sell it. Then I retreat to an alley where I can pretend to nurse my baby.

As expected, a shadow materializes over me. Two orcs appear out of the dark and grab me by the arms, pressing a cloth over my face to muffle my screams. I clutch the bundle close and let them drag me away.

AGKAR

Oh, do I loathe this plan.

It's a good one, but I hate it nonetheless. What no one else knows is that the captain putting herself on the line isn't just risking one life, but two lives, and this knowledge is burning a hole through me.

But I have to acquiesce or risk revealing too much, so I nod my head and agree.

Zirelle plays the part well, I must admit. I watch from behind a ledge as she spends her last few coins. She is a good actress, and I feel a surge of affection for her.

We follow her to the alley, the corporal and I as well as two other officers. As predicted, the attackers materialize and grab her. I know it's all part of the plan, but my protective instinct is like a tidal wave that takes me over all at once. I square my shoulders to go after her, but Corporal Jar'kel holds me back.

"It's not time yet," he says. His eyes narrow. "Control yourself."

We watch them drag her away from the wagon to a darkened doorway down the alley. Once they've vanished inside, we move.

Quietly, carefully, the corporal goes to open the door, but it's locked. Without thinking twice, I pull the door right off its hinges. The other guards stare at me.

"What?" I snarl. "It's efficient."

Lighting our torches, we make our way down the stairs. The room is dark and full of cobwebs. Shelves along the walls contain mostly junk—but most importantly, there's another darkened doorway that leads to yet another set of stairs.

We're headed down again. Promising. This must be a hideout of some kind.

That's when I hear a shriek. I would know that voice anywhere.

I take off down the stairs, despite the corporal calling my name. My baser nature is taking over, and I can't seem to stop my feet as I thunder downward. Nothing will harm my mate as long as I'm alive and breathing.

Suddenly, the narrow stairwell expands into a large room, built out of stone. There are torches hanging along the walls, and as soon as I appear on the stairs, I know that I'll be seen.

"We have company!" a voice calls out. Down below me, I find my Zirelle strapped to a stone slab, the bundle of cloth she used as an infant lying on the floor. She was found out.

A trolless stands over her, with teal blue skin and a mountain of dark red hair, a knife at the ready. I don't hesitate to jump off the stairs and fall the final story to the ground. My legs absorb the shock. I lunge with my sword, and one of the orcs standing guard is immediately in front of me, blocking my attack.

"It's much too late," the trolless calls out, and while I try to force my way past, she holds the dagger up over Zirelle's body. The point of it glimmers in the torchlight.

Then she plunges it in.

"No!" My voice comes out a monstrous roar. I fling the orc to one side and leap past him, and in two strides I'm on top of the trolless. But the damage has already been done, and Zirelle is screaming as the rest of the guard finally joins us. I'm inches away from slicing open the trolless's throat when Corporal Jar'kel stops me.

"We need her alive," he growls. "See to your woman."

I don't think twice about his words as I abandon my kill and head straight for Zirelle. The dagger protrudes from her chest, blood pouring from the wound.

No. No, no, no.

I can't lose her like this.

ZIRELLE

The world is swimming above me. I hear Agkar's voice, but I can't move. Someone pulls me away from the slab. There's yelling and movement all around, but none of it makes sense.

The agony in my chest is unbearable.

Thick arms are carrying me. Something hot and liquid coats my throat, and I'm afraid I'm going to choke on it.

"Hold on," Agkar says to me. "Just hold on."

But I don't know if I can. My mind is drifting away, and the pain is starting to fade. I think of the small being we made together and wish that things had been different. What could life have been like for the three of us? I imagine warm nights exploring the city, stopping occasionally for a tasty treat of cinnamon and syrup. I imagine hot days lying on a bed, Agkar's arm curled around me as our child sleeps between us.

As hard as I try to hold on tight to these dreams, the darkness trickles in, and I fall into it.

CHAPTER 17

AGKAR

She's still breathing when we reach the surface, but barely.

"Healer!" I'm shouting, holding my bleeding mate in my arms in the village square. "Healer!" At least I have some limited Freysian at my disposal. It feels like we wait for an eternity, blood pouring from Zirelle's body, before someone emerges from one of the houses and rushes over. The old man says, "This way," and gestures at the house. I follow him, clutching my mate close to my chest.

When we're inside, the smell of herbs is overwhelming. The man gestures to a bed and I lay her on it, and when I take my hands away, they're covered in blood. My heart almost stops beating.

"Stand back," the corporal says, and tugs me by the shoulder so the man can get access to her. The human brings a cloth to her chest and pulls out the dagger, and her body convulses. As it comes free and blood starts to gush, I've never felt an agony like this in all my life. But the healer is quick and nimble, using every tool at his disposal to staunch the flow. I watch in horror as he works and even more blood dribbles from Zirelle's lips.

She must survive this. If she doesn't, neither will I. The moment she leaves this plane, my soul will break in two, and I'll have no choice but to follow her.

I can't lose them.

Quiet falls in the healer's house as he does everything he can, making poultices and smearing them on the wound. He's saying words like *heart* and *lungs*, and my panic grows, my hands clenched so tight my nails bite into my palms. His words turn into garble.

Corporal Jar'kel's hand lands on my shoulder. "Lieutenant. He says she might live."

Might. I will cling onto that word with everything I have.

When Zirelle's breathing starts to slow, a fresh terror takes hold of me, and all I want is to lift her off the bed and hold her in my arms. She is my heart and my soul and my body. But the corporal forces me to sit in a chair and wait, and then leaves.

I understand, somewhere in the back of my mind, that surely he knows how I feel about the captain who's now lying unconscious, but I can't bring myself to care. We will handle that when she and our whelp make it through this.

The only thing in my vision is my small Zirelle, her chest rising and falling in uneven, shallow heaves while the healer works.

Then she takes in a big, deep breath. When her croaking voice comes out, relief pours through me.

"Agkar?" Her eyes flutter open, and in moments I'm at her side, holding her hand. The old man steps away in surprise. A small smile crosses her face. "Oh, good. It's you."

"It's me." I bring her hand to my lips and try to forget for a moment there's a chance she won't make it. It's just her and me here. She coughs weakly, and some blood coats her mouth. I reach up with my other hand to wipe it away.

"Agkar, I—" She gags again, and I squeeze her hand.

"Don't try to talk," I say. "Just rest."

She wants to object, I know, but she closes her mouth anyway. Her eyes don't leave mine as the healer returns with some new remedy and works on her again. He doesn't make me leave.

It feels like hours have passed when Corporal Jar'kel returns to tell me about the massive reserve of green salt they found. They've cleared out the underground hideout, freeing the hostages and uncovering the store rooms where our perps were making and storing it.

"Your hunch was absolutely correct, Lieutenant," he says. "We've got them." When I don't look up or answer, he says, "If the captain has made it this long, I think she has a good chance."

I hope with every fiber of my being that he's right.

ZIRELLE

I've slipped in and out of consciousness more times than I can count. Each time I'm overwhelmed with pain, and then I disappear into darkness again. But throughout it all is Agkar's voice. I can't make out what he's saying to me, but it's enough to be my lifeline. He is my everything, and I will cling to that with all I have.

I don't know how much time has passed when I can finally open my eyes. The pain is still everywhere, but this time I can actually see. I'm inside a dark clay house, with wood beams holding up the roof. There's an acrid smell, and when I look down to find dark brown blood all across my chest, I realize the smell is me.

Someone is still holding my hand, and when I flex it slightly, I hear Agkar's voice.

"Zirelle?" Soon he's sitting up, and I wonder how long he's been at my bedside.

"Hello," I say, and it comes out a hoarse whisper. A huge smile spreads across his face, lifting his tusks all the way to his eyes, and it's one of the few I've ever seen. I smile back as best I can. He brings a hand up to my face and runs it down to my lips. "How long have I been out?" I ask.

"A few days, on and off." I can tell by the dark lines under his eyes that he's been here at my side the whole time. "But you're going to make it."

Good. I couldn't leave him here alone.

Then ice wraps around my heart. If I was so badly injured, what are the chances that our child survived? I'm afraid to even ask, but quietly, I do. "The baby?"

His big hand strokes my hair. "It lives."

Air rushes back into my lungs, as hard as it is to properly fill them. I could just hug him. Unfortunately, when I try to move at all, a sharp, agonizing pain races through my chest.

"Don't move," a gruff voice says, and an old man approaches me. He shoves Agkar aside, and the big orc growls as he gives the man space. "You're very injured."

"I noticed." I squint at him. "Are you the reason I'm alive?"

He nods. Then he glances down at Agkar, who still hasn't let go of my hand. "And you seem to be clinging to life quite hard. You must have something important to live for."

I think then that it's true. I groan as more pain washes over me.

"Try to rest more," the old healer says. "You need it."

He checks my bandages, and then leaves me alone again. Agkar runs his thumb over my knuckles, over and over, and the gentle motion lulls me back to sleep.

AGKAR

She will live. This thought keeps me afloat every moment. She will keep breathing, and our offspring is safe.

That is all I need.

Corporal Jar'kel obviously knows the truth of what's between us, but I don't think he will talk. We have gotten on well enough since I joined the service, and he seems to respect Zirelle. Soon, though, duty in the city calls, and I can't avoid returning to my position any longer without sacrificing it.

Looking down at my sweet mate, at her rounded stomach rising and falling with her shallow breaths, I wonder if perhaps that's what I should do. It would make one less problem for when she's well again and wants to return to her post. There can be no accusations of an abuse of power if I am no longer her lieutenant.

When I'm certain that Zirelle will be cared for under the supervision of the human healer, I return to the city to tender my resignation in person. I don't know what will come next, but this is the one thing I can do for my woman to make her life easier. Perhaps we still have a chance of keeping our secret. I could care for our whelp and give her a home to come back to, something discreet and quiet that won't sacrifice the work that means so much to her.

As I lay down my lieutenant's coat, I find that I feel nothing. All this time I believed my titles, my achievements, would define my life. I thought that my greatest possessions were ambition and power. Little did I know the purpose of it all would be my beautiful, fearless captain instead.

ZIRELLE

After a lot of prodding and assurances that I'll be all right without him, Agkar leaves my side to return to his duties in Attirex. It is strange after all this time to be without him, and I find that I deeply dislike it. I long for him to hold my hand in his sturdy, four-fingered one. I crave his stern, set face, and the bright eyes shining out from under his sturdy brows as he watches over me, guarding me, protecting me.

My orc, who has been willing to sacrifice so much for me and our child. My orc, who believes in a future that seems far beyond my imagination, who sees a world where we could live our lives together and raise our family together without the confines of the city guard holding us back.

Is that world possible? As I lie there for hours, willing my body to heal faster, I turn it over in my mind again and again.

I've given everything I have to this job. I almost died for it.

Then I think about the little creature growing inside me. Not long from now I'll have a child of my own, just as my parents once did. I imagine Agkar and myself facing off against outlaws, only for our bodies to be discovered, mutilated. I imagine our child alone the way I was, and a heavy pressure builds behind my eyes.

I deserved to be cared for, to have a family who came home to me, just like this one deserves to live without the fear of losing us. After all I've given, don't I deserve that, too?

Corporal Jar'kel has been gathering evidence in preparation for the upcoming trial, and he stops by on his way out of town to see me. We've never been friends, but he seems invested in my survival.

"You're looking better, Captain," Jar'kel says, surveying me. "Your lieutenant will be pleased." So we have not escaped his notice. I wonder if he's told anyone.

I nod in agreement. "I should be back on my feet in a week or two."

"What then?" the corporal asks. His eyes glide over to my belly and back. He's astute for a troll.

My mouth opens and closes again as the words hover on the edge of my lips. I think of all the sweat, all the sleepless nights, the flask in my desk that once helped me get through the day, and how I dread the idea of returning to it.

Would walking away be giving up? Admitting that I couldn't do the job?

I remember the day my parents were found. As a girl I spent a lot of time at our house near the barracks wondering when they would come home. Sometimes I was up until late at night, watching the street from my window so I'd know as soon as they arrived.

But that evening, I stayed up so late I fell asleep leaning on the sill. It wasn't until the knock came at the door, heavy and urgent, that I fully understood something was wrong, and I would never see them again.

"Jar'kel," I begin unsteadily. "Will you bring me my coat?"

He blinks with confusion, then gets up and pads across the healer's house to where my captain's coat is hanging up. Once it's in my lap, I reach for the pin on the breast, the one that tells the world who I am. My captain's pin.

I work it out of the fabric, then offer it to the corporal. He extends his hand to take it.

"Captain?" he asks, brows furrowed. "Are you... resigning?"

"Yes." My resolve is stronger than I expected. In fact, a

burst of hope blooms in my chest as I watch his hand close around the pin and it vanishes from sight. This is the one thing I can give to Agkar, to our child, and to myself. "This position almost cost me everything, and I can't do it anymore."

"If I may?" Jar'kel sits down in Agkar's chair. I gesture to it. "As you like."

"Despite how we felt about one another, you served well and loyally. And that did not come without a price." He glances down at my bandages. "I have never felt the mating bond myself, but I know it when I see it."

All I can do is nod.

"I think you're doing the right thing." He tucks the pin into his pocket. "You've always cared more about this job than it deserves."

"Thank you, Corporal," I say, because I don't know how else to respond to such openness.

Before he departs, Jar'kel pauses at the door to the healer's house and turns back to me. "You should have the life you want, Captain. And so should the lieutenant." Then he's gone.

For the first time in years, my heart feels light, as if some weight I've been carrying my whole life has finally been lifted.

CHAPTER 18

ZIRELLE

I'm surprised when Agkar returns the next day. He's dressed in just a plain tunic and trousers, which looks strange and unfamiliar on him. As usual, the healer makes himself scarce around the big orc. I forget sometimes how intimidating my lieutenant can be if you don't know what's inside him.

"You're back early," I say. "I thought you didn't have a day off until—"

"I'm done," he interrupts. Agkar sits beside me, in the chair that's become his, and clasps his hand around mine.

"What do you mean?" Even his hair is down, hanging loose to one side of his head.

"I left the service." He pats his chest, where his own Lieutenant's pin would normally reside. "No more risk."

A stone drops in my stomach. "You... you gave it up?" I can't help it this time when the tears gather in my eyes. This business about making a new person has been awful for keeping my emotions in check.

He squeezes my hand and leans over me, as if protecting me with his big body. "Of course. The city guard is your life, all you've ever worked for. I don't want you to have to choose." Then Agkar notices that tears are blooming in my eyes, and his eyebrows draw together. "What's wrong?"

I don't know if they're sad or happy tears, or perhaps a mixture of both.

My Agkar. My mate. He gave up everything.

"Nothing," I say finally. He wipes one of the many tears away from my face. "Nothing is wrong at all."

I tell him what I've done, and he gapes at me. "But it meant everything to you."

"No." I shake my head. "It was a prison, Agkar. It has been since before I ever joined. Even if this hadn't happened..." I wind our hands together and run them over my belly. "Someday I would have had to look at my reflection in the mirror and realize that I was killing myself slowly." I can't help but smile. "Now I can live the way I want."

"Zirelle." His voice is thick. I slide over on the bed so he can lie down next to me, and his heart is beating so fast I worry it might jump out of his chest. "You are a wonder," he whispers, nuzzling my face between his tusks. "Always surprising me."

"In a good way?"

He chuckles, kissing the top of my head. "Most of the time."

It's another two weeks before the healer lets me go. He's been paid for his services by the city of Attirex, but it's the last time I'll receive any favors.

The old man's happy to see us leave, and I think Agkar made him quite uncomfortable. My orc is an imposing figure, I'll give him that.

"Where should we go?" I ask as we step out into the harsh sunlight of the Hazrain.

"Where do you want to go?" Agkar puts an arm around my waist, tugging me closer.

"Attirex is my home," I say. "I don't know anything else." I can't imagine trying to settle in a place that isn't my vast, oppressive, wonderful desert. Perhaps it's not for everyone, but it's what I know. I only hope that Agkar will agree, as much as he once hated it here.

"Then we'll return there," he says amiably. "I'll find work. It's a big city." He doesn't look displeased by this idea at all—if anything, there's a mischievous smile hovering on the edge of his mouth, something I've never seen before. I would almost think he's happy with the way this has all worked out.

My handsome orc is resourceful and steadfast. I know together we can see it through.

All we can afford on our meager coin is a small room above a merchant's shop, just big enough for the two of us and the little one. Agkar takes odd jobs here and there as he can find them, and we manage while I recover at home. I almost don't recognize this orc who came to the Hazrain so many months ago.

Unfortunately, by the time I'm well enough to work again, I'm huge around the middle and it's difficult for me to get around. Every night, Agkar returns home and pulls me down into bed with him. He sucks my nipples and runs his hands all over my swollen belly. He licks me between the legs and then takes me slowly, gently, and I moan and cry out until the merchant bangs on the ceiling.

"You're going to carry so many of my whelps," he groans into my ear. "Until we have a whole horde of them."

"Who's going to take care of all those little orcs?" I ask, gasping as he strokes in and out of me. It surely won't be me.

"Just you wait until you see what a damn good father I am," he growls into my ear. "Then you'll never ask that again."

Soon, I just want this damn baby out of me. I'm pretty sure I've gotten bigger than any human should be, and it makes it difficult just to walk. Agkar hovers every moment that he's not working.

"What if we weren't supposed to do this?" I ask with a groan as I turn over in bed to lie on my side. "I don't know how much longer I can wait."

He rubs along my back, working out the knots above my hips. It's a wonder to me every day how that stubborn, arrogant, impertinent orc who first came into my employ has become my beloved and attentive mate. I'd never craved tenderness before, but perhaps I didn't know what tenderness could be.

Often I think of the carvings of two faces, human and trollkin, looking deeply into one another's eyes, and feel that it understood something I didn't—not until now.

At first, I'm relieved when I go into labor, but it's not long before I feel a pain even worse than getting stabbed in the chest. I grit my teeth, as I always have. Agkar is there with me, gripping my hand, describing the life we'll live in my ear while I sob.

Eventually I do make it through without splitting in half. It's Agkar who brings the screaming infant over to me. She's olive green, like him, and has one cute little tuft of black hair. Her eyes are the same bright gold-green as his.

Pure orc, through and through.

Agkar adjusts the pillows as I sit up so I can bring her to my nipple. Her little gums bite down and I grimace. "Damn. Maybe having a baby with an orc was a mistake."

Agkar just laughs. I remember the heartsick look he had in his eyes once upon a time, and wonder if perhaps we were always meant to find each other.

I hope I hear him laugh many more times.

AGKAR

Once my Zirelle is recovered enough to be up and about again, it's not long before she's looking for work. There's a bright optimism in her face as she contemplates what sort of job she'd like to do, what would draw on her talents and keep her interested.

She was never destined for mothering, I know that. I knew it the moment I bonded with her, and even then, I had accepted my role. I was always meant for her, and she for me. As difficult as it's been, I wouldn't trade this journey for the world.

When our whelp Keza is old enough to be without her mother, Zirelle finds a short-term job working as private security for a human dignitary visiting Attirex. It's a job that requires both delicacy and strength, and she's perfect for it. Soon she lands more work protecting a merchant caravan across the desert, helping to bring supplies and commerce in and out of the city. Sometimes it takes her away for days, even weeks at a time, and it's just me and Keza exploring the beautiful, sweet-smelling city together. She loves to grab my hair and chew on it while she sits on my shoulders, and she cries miserably when her little tusks come in. I carry an affection for her I never thought possible, but one I think I've always craved.

Once in the market I run into Corporal Jar'kel patrolling the city. We exchange nods, but when he sees Keza, he cracks a smile.

Most of the time my mate makes me pull out right at the end, but it isn't terribly long before she gets the urge again. She can't resist the call of the bond, either, so I bury myself as deep as I can in her warm, beautiful cunt, and fill her up with my seed, excited for what will come out next.

It may not look exactly like the life either of us had expected for ourselves, but I find I don't miss my old one, not for a moment. Every day my Zirelle is happier than the day before it, happier than I ever thought she could be, in control of her own destiny. She comes home every night and kisses Keza on the forehead, then tucks herself into my arms right where she belongs.

My captain is everything I could have wanted, and so much more.

THANK YOU FOR READING!

If you enjoyed this book, please consider leaving a review! Written reviews help authors like me reach new readers.

JOIN MY NEWSLETTER!

For all the latest regarding books, and to get a FREE novelette that takes place in the Trollkin Lovers universe, sign up for my newsletter!

www.LyonneRiley.com

Also by Lyonne Riley

Trollkin Lovers

Stealing the Troll's Heart

Healing the Orc's Heart

Tempting the Ogre's Heart

Standalones

Prince of Beasts

The Monster Menagerie

ABOUT THE AUTHOR

I come from a traditional publishing background, which is rewarding but often too rigid, so I shifted to self-publishing to pursue my real passion in writing: extremely sexy monster romance. I probably should have known I would end up here after spending most of my young adulthood writing erotic fan fiction, but it took me a while to find my way back to myself.

ACKNOWLEDGMENTS

I would like to thank everyone involved in helping me through the process of putting out this book. I can't say enough how much I appreciate the help and encouragement of the people around me—especially Amber, who told me I could do this in the first place.

Huge thank you to Rowan Woodcock for the beautiful cover illustration. And to my critique partners, Ruth, Ash, and Kassie, who gave me phenomenal editorial feedback: You all make this possible. And of course, my amazing spouse, who has always supported my dreams—and given me lots of inspiration for my characters' sexy adventures.

I couldn't have done this without the expertise of my fellow self-published romance authors. Thank you for inviting me into your circles and helping me through this process.

And thank you to my readers, who gave this book a shot.

Made in the USA
Middletown, DE
05 May 2024

53872157R00089